To Carolyn & Cap
love

SAILING HOME

Jim

April 20, 1982

Also by Cynthia King

IN THE MORNING OF TIME
THE YEAR OF MR. NOBODY
BEGGARS AND CHOOSERS

SAILING HOME

CYNTHIA KING

G.P. PUTNAM'S SONS, NEW YORK

This book is wholly fiction. Any resemblance to persons living or dead, or to actual events, is entirely coincidental.

Acknowledgments:
I would like to thank more friends than there is space to mention. Especially, my agent, Pat Berens; my editor, Margaret Frith; Lois and Chuck Thomsen, sailing companions through fair and foul weather. And I would like to thank JK for many gifts: among them his patience, encouragement, and critical judgment, not to mention sailing lessons and help with the nomenclature.

Library of Congress Cataloging in Publication Data
King, Cynthia.
Sailing home.
Summary: After two years traveling with a
hippie family eighteen-year-old Paul returns
home to finish school and to go sailing
again with the girl friend whose father's
false accusations had caused him to run away.
[1. Runaways—Fiction. 2. Sailing—Fiction.
3. Hippies—Fiction] I. Title.
PZ7.K5758Sai 1982 [Fic] 81–22711
ISBN 0-399-20872-0 AACR2

For CLARA
and also for
NATHANIEL and JEAN

SAILING HOME

ONE

Paul tucked the tiller under his arm and felt the good breeze freshen. The mainsheet pulled taut in his hand. The Ensign heeled deliciously as he pressed his weight against the smooth laminated wood of the combing and swung the bow close to the wind. He'd gotten off the mooring without a hitch, cleared the small boats in the harbor. He felt relieved, deeply refreshed, as he always had with the wind and water neatly in the power of his two hands. He grinned at Mary Lou across from him.

"You look fine," he said.

"Oh? Do I?" Her eyes shone.

He ran his bare toe along the ragged edge of her cut-off jeans, teasing. She didn't move her leg away, just wet her lips and watched him.

She looked older than he remembered. She didn't flinch at the touch as she would have two years ago. But the sun-bleached hair was the same, still blowing out of control until she rummaged in her ditty bag for a rubber band and pulled it back. He used to wonder why she never did that until they were under way, until the wind caught the straight strands, tangled them in the rigging, blinded her or caught in her mouth. Perhaps she wanted him to see it, pale silk in the sunlight, before she tucked it away.

The planes of her face were squarer now, her cheekbones sharper, lips fuller, though she still wore no makeup. Her tan wind-smoothed cheeks reminded him of the desert in the afternoon. He remembered a crooked cactus behind which two lizards played.

"Sometimes I couldn't remember what you looked like," he said.

"Oh? What did you remember?"

"You liked Baby Ruths. Junk food. And you didn't like to wear your glasses, so you squinted a lot."

"Oh! I'd forgotten. I hate that stuff now."

"But you still don't wear your glasses."

"I have contacts."

"I'd never have guessed."

"I'm not wearing them now! Not out here! What else?"

"And the way you seemed to apologize for being there. Some girls were pushy. You were wide-eyed, half-scared, but you really wanted to learn. You were a good listener."

"Oh!" she said softly.

"And the different ways you said 'Oh.' You must have twenty or more. It can mean anything."

She blushed.

"You didn't know you did that?"

"Oh!" She turned her head away, fake mad.

He laughed. So far, so good. Maybe they could keep going from the moment they'd left each other, just keep sailing. He could still affect her. She'd always been easy to tease. Maybe coming home hadn't been such a mistake after all.

He relaxed, allowing himself to feel in his throat and chest that fullness of being on the Sound with her again: wind, water, sun, and salt; silence but for the lapping of waves on the hull, the now-and-then creak of the keel, the twing of the stays, and the tightrope of emotion between them.

He heard the mournful bell before he saw it. The big

10

genoa jib blocked his view. He ducked his head, looked under the "genny," got the bell's position, and shifted course so he'd leave it to starboard. Once past, he would head off shore toward the Island. A swim would be good; if the wind held, he might make it to Oyster Bay and Cold Spring Harbor.

He knew these markers in the great body of water that was Long Island Sound as well as he knew the signs on Barrow Street where he grew up, or the feel of the living-room rug under his bare feet, and his mother's voice, "If I trip over your shoes, Paul, one more time . . ."

The bell rang again. On a foggy night the sound was dull, hard to place, calling to him, tricky like his brother Joe—six years older than he—a giant playing hide and seek. Joe was still tricky, pretending not to recognize him when he rang the doorbell last year in California. Looking for Joe so far from home, trying to survive these last two years, had been like sailing through a dense fog.

Sailing was easier. He'd been doing that nearly all his life here in Rocky Shores and summers with his grandfather Jojo on Cape Cod. The deep gong of the harbor bell had sometimes come into his dreams, calling him, showing him the way home. Often enough in the last year, trying to sleep on some strange and filthy floor, the sound sliced knifelike into his sleep, slitting the leather skin he had tried to clothe his soft psyche in. At the sound of that bell, the skin would part, and a terrible loneliness would sweep in like a cold wind in a new wound. Sometimes, trying to be what he was and do what he did and the rest be damned, he felt betrayed by the bell. Sometimes in the nightmares he would cover his ears with his hands, trying to deafen himself to the resonant ring.

Today, the first time on any boat in two years, and Mary Lou with him, rather than comforting, the bell reminded him of the distance between them that time had created.

11

To cross the distance he said, "Remember the night we got fogged up in Greenwich and didn't get home until three A.M.?"

"Do I!" She shivered and hugged her knees. "I was grounded for a month."

Testing her further, he said, "You thought your parents would worry about your drowning. Remember? But it was your virginity they cared about." Two years ago he wouldn't have used that word with her. She didn't seem to notice.

"Not even that. My reputation."

He laughed.

"You can laugh. You didn't have to live with them." Her voice suddenly sounded like hitting two sticks of wood together. He looked up startled. She was squinting.

"Do they know I'm back?" he asked. "Did you tell them who mans the vacuum at the carwash?"

What he really meant but couldn't say was: Do they know where I've been? What I've done? Do *you* know? Can I come home again?

Before she could answer, the boat heeled sharply as a puff filled the sail. The sheet slid through his fingers. Caught off balance, he grabbed the tiller and pulled the sail in tight. He nodded for Mary Lou to come up to the high side and help him level out. He was embarrassed. He should have seen that puff coming.

"Take the jib sheet," he said, all captain again. She braced her feet against the seat on the low side and wrapped the Dacron line around her hand.

They rode out the puff, enjoying it as the Ensign heeled just right and sliced into the wind. He grinned at her, shoulder to shoulder with him now. "You're good crew," he said. "Haven't forgotten. You sailed much lately?"

"Not once since you left." She flipped her hair back.

He was pleased, he thought. But then, what had she done

while he'd been gone? What had she done, and with whom?

He studied the changes in her face. Some were simple signs of growing up—she'd only been fourteen then. But was there a hardness to her jaw now that matched that hard-edged voice? He wasn't sure how, but she wasn't the same.

Well, neither was he.

"Ease off on the jib," he said, and let out the main as they came around the bell. The boat leveled when he changed course. "We'll reach across."

"Where are we going?" she asked.

Suddenly the anger he had suppressed rose up, sour like bile. "I don't know about you," he said, unable to control his harsh and belligerent tone, "but I figure on a swim at Matinicock Point. If the wind holds"—he eyed her carefully—"we might make it to Cold Spring Harbor."

He shifted his weight and created an air space between them. He trimmed the sheet and set his course. She cleated the jib sheet, then slid along the seat and leaned against the cuddy, tucking her knees up to her chest. She closed her eyes and hung her hand over the side, dipping her fingertips now and then.

He wished he hadn't let his anger show. He'd hoped they could talk again. He wished he could apologize. He couldn't. If only she hadn't asked that question. Any question.

What was she thinking behind those closed eyes?

Your shoulder is hard against my arm, and the jib sheet feels like a wrestler's handgrip. No, I'm not frightened, but it's strange remembering the last time you touched me. There was nothing hard about you then. Your jaw was soft and your skin was smooth, your legs brown and hairless.

13

Yet each time your hand reached for mine, something made me pull back, repulsed. No, not repulsed, but irritated. Frightened. You always wanted to touch me. Everything embarrassed me: the way you looked at me; the way I couldn't help feeling about you. I didn't want to be in love yet. I just wanted to have fun, go sailing, do daring things. Now your jaw is like iron and your nose is big and you've got blond stubble on your face. Your legs are thick and scabbed, and I can see dark hairs where your shirt is open. But now you don't frighten me. I liked the feeling of your leg touching mine. All that summer I dreamed of you kissing me, but when you tried, I hated you for it. Ever since you left, I've dreamed of you doing it again.

The first kiss is the scariest. The second one is easier. The first kiss. The first drink. The first joint. The first time you say damn or hell or . . .

Where are we going?

What's so wrong about asking that? It's just something to say. It doesn't matter. I don't care where. You didn't used to be so sensitive. I never saw you angry. You're changed, Paul. I want to know where you've been and what you've done, but I don't dare ask.

TWO

Where are we going? Where are we going? She might as well have asked where the wind was going, or a wave. Who the hell knew where they were going, if anywhere, together or apart? And what did it matter? If only he could live just one day without having to hear that question.

It had driven him west two years before. Spoken or unspoken, it was driving him crazy in his mother's house now. That question had made him get the sails to Jojo's boat out of the cellar, say ever so casually last night, "Mind if I take the Ensign out tomorrow?" Knowing that Jojo wouldn't say if he minded. But also knowing that if anyone said "Where are you going?" he might never bring it back.

Paul watched Mary Lou settle herself against the cuddy and close her eyes. Good, he could watch her without having to talk. He could wait till he cooled. He focused on her knees, her throat, the corn silk blowing across her lips, then on the telltale fluttering from the shroud two feet over her head, then finally on the dark line of the North Shore. As his anger seeped away, his depression returned. He'd survived without anger for two years. Now in a few short weeks he was pushing it down all the time. He had no reason to be mad at Mary Lou, but in that quick reaction he'd lumped her in with the others.

Maybe he shouldn't have invited her out, or "borrowed" the Ensign, or even come home.

Suddenly he saw not Mary Lou but Ellie, her braids lying across her green flowered balloon dress. "Love is irrelevant." He shook his head to clear it. His mind had tricked him again. It scared him not to be able to control what he remembered, what he forgot.

You'd sail your life away. You can't drift forever, Paul. You spend mighty little time hitting those books. You're a junior now, ought to be looking at colleges. Take the SATs next Saturday. Get plenty of sleep. Another ticket! You'll lose your license. Joe got straight A's; he chose where he went to college. What do you want to be, Paul?

Want! His mother didn't care what he wanted, only the work he did. She hadn't always been that way. She'd changed; everyone and everything had changed the year his father died. When the cancer grew in Dad, it seemed as if Mom, Joe, and the whole world got sick and everyone Paul cared about left.

It started in fourth grade, when Matty Nagle, his best friend since kindergarten, moved away—under a cloud, Mom said, because his father was in some kind of trouble. But Mom never had liked Matty much. Matty promised to write, but Paul never heard from him. And he never had another friend like him.

He tried hanging around Joe, but it didn't work out. Joe was either holed up in his room studying—he was applying for early admission to college—or surrounded by his pack of friends. To them Paul was Joe's cute little brother, good for a laugh or an errand. "Get us a couple of beers from the fridge, Paulie. Don't tell Dad. . . ." He was glad to do it.

Dad and Joe were always at each other that year. "If you spent more time studying and less time demonstrating, you might make some difference in the world," Dad would say when Joe came home too late.

"Everything I do is wrong, according to you." Joe would

16

stamp up to his room. Mom would try to calm Dad down. "If he isn't idealistic now, he never will be," she'd say.

"Idealistic!" Dad would rant. "He's antiparent, antiestablishment, antieverything but his own pleasure." The arguments raged on.

The house was peaceful after Joe left for college. Dad talked to Paul as he never had before. "Funny kid, your brother," he said once. "Wants to save the world but he can't get on with his own family." Paul made a point of getting on with everyone, especially Dad. But then suddenly, too soon, Dad got sick.

During those next hard months Paul and his mother were close. He'd leave school early so she could keep the afternoon shift at the library. There were many days they didn't dare leave Dad alone even for an hour, and then so many trips to the hospital. Everyone was proud of Paul. He was such a help. "You don't have to come home," Mom told Joe on the phone. "Paul's here."

He was glad when Jojo decided to live with them after Dad died. He'd spent whole summers with Jojo. But that didn't work out as he expected either. He couldn't explain that he'd been the man of the house, he wasn't a little kid anymore. He couldn't take orders from Jojo here the way he had on the Cape. He didn't need a second father. And he was embarrassed to remember crawling into the old man's lap to watch shooting stars over Cape Cod Bay.

But Paul kept the atmosphere in the house nice. He and Jojo talked about boats, about summers past; Jojo talked about the community his grandfather had built, and about Paul's mother as a little girl, about Cape Cod the way it used to be before the new road went in and it got so crowded. Paul listened, but it had nothing to do with him. Jojo couldn't fill the hollow inside him.

The problem was, right after the funeral his mother seemed to retreat. While they sat around the living room

17

awkwardly with some friends and neighbors, someone said, "Good boy, Paul. Your mother really needs you now." He looked across the room at Mom—she sat straight up in the wing chair, her hands tight in her lap. He couldn't think of anything to do for her. Dad was dead. There wasn't anything to do together anymore.

She'd always been close to Joe, taking his side in arguments when Dad was angry. But now she seemed angry at him too, almost as if she blamed him for Dad's death. Joe offered to stay home, but Mom insisted he go back to California. She said, "Your education is the best way you can repay him, Joe. But remember, it's his money that's putting you through. . . ."

Joe shrugged, gave Paul a ten-dollar bill, patted him on the shoulder, and said, "Take care, Paulie."

A few months later Paul woke in the night, reaching, calling, still half in that dream he hated, where Dad was alive but falling out of bed, so heavy, slipping out of his hands. Paul must have yelled out loud, because her voice was cool from the doorway.

"What is it, Paul? Did you call?"

"I don't know." He didn't remember crying out. He'd been embarrassed to admit he'd had a nightmare, even wet his bed a little. After all, he was twelve, old enough to get himself up in the night.

The cool voice from the doorway said, "All right, then. I've got to get some sleep. Have to be at the library early." She was head librarian now and worked full time.

But why did she expect him to stop acting like a kid? She leaned on him; he felt her weight. He didn't mind helping her take care of the house, but he didn't see why he shouldn't laugh. If your father died, did you have to be serious forever? She got after him about things nobody worried about before.

She actually got up from the dinner table in a huff one

night saying, "You two never talk about anything. Boats. Cars. Don't you ever think, Paul, or read a book? I found two, six months overdue at the library, under your bed last week. So dusty you couldn't have read them."

"I forgot they were there," he'd said miserably. It was true. He'd check books out, get bored after a few pages, and never finish them. He didn't think reading was better than other things to do. He liked talking boat talk with his grandfather. He was almost old enough to drive. He thought about that. He caught her looking at him with something like loathing, as if she were thinking: Why are you alive when he is dead?

A couple of days later Jojo and he were washing dishes. Jojo said, "You know, Paul, you're getting to look a lot like your dad. I think it upsets your mother."

Paul didn't know what to say, so he didn't say anything. He couldn't help the way he looked, or the way he was either.

It got heavy after that, especially after he got his license. You want to borrow the car? After you mow. Take the boat out? Have you cleaned the cellar, done your homework, emptied the garbage, fixed the shutter? Even the mail dogged him—another overdue notice from the library, a failing slip in math. His teacher said, "You're not a bit like your brother Joe, are you? He was a real mathematician."

"You used to be so sweet, Paul," his mother said. "Now you're off in your own world. You never talk to me anymore. I can't get through." But if he told her anything, she criticized him. He couldn't remember touching her since she held his hand when they walked into the mausoleum.

That was a long, long time back.

Since then he'd met Mary Lou, and lost her; he'd gone across a desert, and now come home. *You're letting things slip, Paul. . . . You lost your camera. . . . You're crazy.*

19

Was he crazy? A drifter? Or worse? Would those names thrown at him on that worst of nights cling to him forever?

But the worst of nights had also been the best, he remembered. The fog had closed in on him and Mary Lou while they were still off Greenwich, isolating them, changing them.

Paul had taken a couple of oranges, some Cokes, and picked her up right after breakfast. He heard her mother's objections as he stood on the back steps.

"Who else is going?"

"Oh, Mother, I don't know. All the kids in the sailing club. It's a race, the last one of the summer."

"Be home by five."

"If the wind doesn't die."

"I don't like you and Paul being alone on the boat."

"It only holds two people. Any more and we'd sink."

Her father said she was too young to go out with him, so the sailing club was the only way Paul could be with her. The family had moved up from a small town in East Texas the year before, where, Mary Lou told him, the most exciting thing all year was when the cheerleaders marched down Main Street before the big game.

The first day of Charley's sailing class, Paul noticed her right away. She was skinny, like a little girl, standing straight and stiff in red shorts and a white shirt. The other girls were sloppy. She listened hard to every word Charley said.

Paul worked for Charley, and since Mary Lou was a brand-new sailor, he had to teach her everything. She'd never seen salt water, tides, seaweed, barnacles. Everything amazed, scared, and fascinated her. It was July before she quit worrying about what was swimming with her in that murky, choppy Sound.

"The thing about sailing," Charley explained the first

20

day, "is that whatever you learn in order to be a good sailor is a lesson in living." Some of the little boys yawned. "Sure, you have to memorize a lot of names of parts of a boat. That's so when you're in a tight spot your crew will understand your orders.

"You can't waste time screwing around with long explanations," he told them. "*Hard alee* means that the boom is going to slam over the boat and the crew better duck or get wiped out. It makes better sense to say 'Hard alee' than to say 'Look out!' because that doesn't tell you what to look out for. It could be another boat in the way, or a wave, or anything.

"In a race if somebody yells, 'Starboard!' that means they've got the right of way and your boat is crossing their path.

"Learning how to make those fast decisions, how to measure the wind, how to know just how far to let the boat heel, all those little niggly things, is like getting through the toughest test of all. Getting knowledge, then using it," he said. "Keeping alert. The dynamics of sailing is a lesson in physics."

By this time three of the boys were playing Scissors, Paper, and Rock, and the girls, except for Mary Lou, were whispering.

He ended up with, "People who sail well can't be bad. That's why no one can board a boat who doesn't know the nomenclature."

Everyone groaned.

Mary Lou learned fast. By the end of the first morning she knew a sheet from a halyard, port from starboard, a cleat from a shackle, but she was hopeless with knots. At the end of a week, when she still couldn't tie a bowline, Paul stood behind her, reaching around the way Jojo taught him to tie a necktie. He thought he'd never met a girl with silkier hair. He thought maybe if her hair weren't in her eyes she'd be able to see how to form the loop. Suddenly afraid of what he was thinking, he dropped the Dacron and said, "You'd better get a book."

"Some teacher," she said, but he saw she was smiling.

He told her a seat was a "thwart" and back was "astern" and "off" meant away from the wind.

She told him her little brother Jamie was jealous because her father said he was too young to sail.

"I started when I was one," Paul said, "in my dad's arms in my grandfather's boat."

She told him her father hadn't wanted to move east but his company made him. Her mother still missed their neighbors back home and thought people here weren't friendly.

"So you're the lucky one in the family," he said.

"Oh?" She opened her eyes wide. "I guess I am."

The next day she came to the dock holding a perfect bowline. "I learned how from a book," she said.

"Where'd you get it?" he asked, surprised.

"The library. There's a whole shelf on sailing. A person could learn everything without getting near a boat."

"I doubt that." But he was impressed. "That's the best thing I've heard about the library. My mother would be pleased. She works there."

"Oh? You mean you're ordinary enough to have a mother?"

He caught his breath. Nobody'd ever suggested that he wasn't ordinary before. He walked her home that day, and on the way in picked up the two empty garbage cans the trash collectors had left on the path.

"Thank you," Mrs. Siddons said when she saw what he'd done. "You're a big help." She was a pale woman with blond hair puffed up pretty high.

"I come from a long line of helpers," he said. "My great-grandmother helped my great-great-grandfather, and my grandfather helps my mother, and I'm supposed to take out the garbage and bring in the cans, so . . ."

Mary Lou giggled and introduced him.

Then, since things were going well, he asked Mrs. Siddons if Mary Lou could go to the movies with him.

She hesitated, then said they had a rule, but she'd ask Mr. Siddons about some other night. Mary Lou's face turned pink.

The next day Mary Lou explained that she wasn't allowed to go out with boys till she was sixteen. She studied her bare feet.

"Don't they trust you?" The words slipped off his tongue. "Sorry," he mumbled, suddenly realizing it was probably him they didn't trust. "I mean, it seems kind of strange."

"Don't you have any rules you have to obey?" she asked. They were still in the clubhouse, while the rest of the class was already down by the water.

"It works differently," Paul said. "My grandfather Jojo has a philosophy. He talks about it a lot. His father grew up in a kind of ideal community upstate. There were a lot of rules, like a man had to have responsibility. Everyone worked at something, and it was for the good of the whole community. In our house, because Mom works full time, Jojo and I share the housework. He cooks and cleans, and I help. Nobody talks about rules, and nobody seems to worry about what I do."

"You're lucky," she said.

That wasn't quite true, so he added, "Only what I *don't* do."

"Hey, Tex," Charley called. "You going to stand there gassing all day? You'll miss the breeze. Paul, I need you here. Come rig this boat."

In June and September, Long Island Sound could be great sailing, with brisk winds, plenty rough and exciting. But in July and August it was often a steam bath.

By midsummer Charley let some of the young sailors single-hand their boats, but Mary Lou never wanted to, even in a light wind. Paul nearly always sailed with her. They'd be alone for whole afternoons. Whenever he made her take the tiller, she'd be tense and serious, squinting, biting her lip, asking a million questions. Every time they passed a buoy she'd want to know what it meant. "Should I go close or stay away?" she'd ask. "Tell me what to do."

He explained the water signposts: bells designated the harbors; red and black striped spars obstructions—a pile of rocks or a wreck. "Stay clear of those," he told her. "The black can and red nun buoys are channel markers. Cans are flat and nuns are conical. Always remember, red right returning. Keep the nun to starboard when you're going home, the can to port. Reverse it when you're heading out. If you stay between them you can't run aground."

"Red right returning," she repeated. "But why call that thing a nun?"

He shrugged. "Habit," I guess.

He explained how to watch the luff on the mainsail so she could judge when to steer off the wind. Once she was so intent on watching the sail, he let her ram right into another boat. There wasn't enough wind to hurt anything, but she was furious.

"Why didn't you warn me?" she cried. "What kind of a teacher are you?"

He grinned. "You won't forget to look ahead again," he said. That was the kind of lesson his dad used to give him, he told her. "Let me fall down a manhole if I was dumb enough not to look."

"If I look ahead now," she said, "all I see is a big blank in your future. Here." She handed him the sheet and went forward, sitting on the deck with her back to him. He liked watching her moods change. Daring one minute, wanting to heel over and hike way out; scared the next; he even liked her angry.

24

By midsummer he thought they knew everything about each other. He told her about his father. "We were going to walk the continental divide together when I got to be sixteen," Paul said. "Even when he knew he was dying and could hardly hold up his hand, he'd pretend and talk about it."

"How old are you now?" she asked.

"Sixteen."

"I used to be close to my father too," she said. "He'd take me walking on Sundays, just the two of us. We'd go for miles in those woods. You wouldn't believe how tall those trees are, pine mostly, but oak too. And yaupon grows underneath and catches the dead pine needles. Daddy carried his gun, but he never used it. We'd sit on a log and he'd make me be quiet. Then we'd listen to the forest noises for the longest time."

"Aren't you close to him now?"

She shrugged. "We don't do anything. He treats me differently, complains to my mother about what I wear."

"You look all right to me," Paul said, meaning a lot more.

"Back home," she said, "some kids dropped out of school and did dope. They hung out in the motorcycle shop behind a garage. My father tried to get them run out of town. He warned me to stay away from them. He didn't need to. They weren't very interesting. He's worse here."

"How so?"

"He thinks communists and junkies lurk in every alley. He hates New York and worries about getting mugged. He doesn't even like Mom going to town alone. He's put double locks on the doors and keeps his gun where he can get at it."

"My dad grew up in New York. It's a great place. Maybe you could go in with me . . . well, sometime."

Mary Lou studied her hand. "He thinks eastern kids are too sophisticated. Drink and smoke today, burn the house down tomorrow."

"Aren't people just people, the same everywhere? There are good ones and bad ones in any place," Paul said.

She brushed her hair out of her eyes. "I only know two places. It's different here. Last winter I didn't know what the girls in my class were talking about half the time."

By midsummer the kids in the sailing class assumed they were a couple. For the first time in years, Paul wasn't lonely. They'd talk on the phone while they watched the same TV show. Almost as good as going to a movie. One night Mary Lou surprised him, calling from a house where she was baby-sitting. He went over after the baby was asleep. They laughed about what her parents would say if they knew, though all they did was watch a movie. He didn't even hold her hand. He thought of it. He felt like a trespasser all the time he was there.

"How long till you're sixteen?" he asked.

"Too long," she said.

He reached for her hand. She jerked it away as if he held a live wire. In the boat they'd touch accidentally and she'd move or make some excuse to go forward. He wanted to touch her, to brush the hair from her eyes, to trace the outline of her cheek with his finger. He'd never felt like that with anyone before.

"Maybe your father's right. If we went to a movie, I'd want to hold your hand. You'd hate that."

"Maybe," she said.

He didn't know whether she meant about her parents being right or about her hating him to hold her hand. He watched the light from the TV tube flicker on her face.

Now, two years later, close to her again but so far apart, he studied the hand that dipped and dipped in the waves, that hand he had finally held. And he wondered what would have happened to them if he hadn't wanted to touch her so much. If her father had let her go out with him. If they hadn't sailed to Greenwich. If . . . if . . . if . . .

Last week you were nothing but a dream, a memory. Something that happened when I was a kid. A fairy tale— the Lost Prince.

Suddenly you were standing by the window of my car holding a vacuum hose. You were opening my door. A mirage? A miracle!

I was so dumb and tongue-tied. It was August when you left, August when you came back. Had time stopped? Had anything happened in between? You grinned, and I thought you were going to tease me. Suddenly I was fourteen again, mad at my father for not letting me go to the movies with you.

You asked if I remembered sailing to Greenwich. Stupid! A day that changes your whole life isn't something you forget. Now knowing you're watching me, wondering what you are wondering, how much you remember, everything comes back, each minute, each sound, every feeling.

I was excited from the moment you came to the door. I was dying to get out of the house. I'd had a terrible fight the night before with Mother and Daddy. I never told you that. I was ashamed of it, but angry too that they were so strict and small-town. Things you'd told me about your family made me know how narrow mine was. You used to tell me nothing was black and white, but all wonderful shades. To them everything was black and white, straight or crooked, right or wrong. But I hadn't meant to fight with them either. It happened over nothing. Jamie spilled some soup and Daddy got too mad. I said good table manners never got me anything I wanted, like the right to see a friend in the evening. I hated him picking on Jamie.

27

Daddy slammed his hand down on the table so hard his own soup spilled.

"Talk about manners," I said under my breath.

"Your so-called friend has corrupted you already," Daddy said. "Taught you to disrespect your own father."

He meant you, Paul, and he hadn't even met you.

THREE

Paul had sensed a difference in Mary Lou the minute he picked her up. He chalked it up to being the last race of the summer, the last day of sailing class, perhaps their last chance to be together.

When they arrived at the dock, Charley was assigning boats. He winked at them. "I really shouldn't let you two experts pair off. Unfair competition." He wrinkled his already wrinkled forehead. "At least, not without a handicap."

Paul held his breath. He didn't want a passenger.

"Take number eight." Charley grinned. "Slowest boat we've got." Oh, excellent. They always sailed number eight.

On a good west wind they passed the first mark with only one other boat in sight. At that speed they'd be through before noon, Paul figured. So they ducked the race, just sailed by the mark. The little Blue Jay planed all the way to Greenwich harbor.

"We'll be back long before the last of the slowpokes finish," Paul said.

"So long as you know the way," Mary Lou said, facing the wind while she tied back her hair. "It's fine with me." Then, imitating her mother, "Be home by five." Then she laughed.

"If the wind doesn't die," he said.

They dropped anchor in one of the small bays out of line of harbor traffic and swam gloriously for hours.

Paul threw a line off the stern cleat and they held to it, letting themselves be tugged in the swift outgoing tide. They accidentally touched—more than once—while they fooled around in the water. Once he almost kissed her, tasting salt water on her lips. She didn't act scared that day.

She swam around the boat, he remembered; he raced after her. She was a child, laughing, teasing, playing a game. When she caught the stern line again, he caught her and this time kissed her harder. He felt shock waves go through her body, and through his own. Suddenly this was no game. Something had happened.

Suddenly he realized the sun was too low and the tide had turned. The boat swung around. The water that rushed past them now was cold. They climbed on board, and Paul hurried to pull up the sails. Already the wind was dropping.

"You take the helm," Mary Lou said. "I can't seem to find the wind. Which tack are we supposed to be on?"

He took the helm, but the sail hung limp. He had to get clear of the land to pick up wind and be helped by the tide, not pushed back. He lifted a floorboard and used it as a paddle.

Mary Lou stood on the foredeck waving at the motor-boats that churned by. None stopped. She was near tears.

"You'd think one of them would see us. All they do is knock the wind out of our sails." The motion of the stalled boat was making her sick.

"Don't even wave. They see us."

"Why don't we have a motor?"

"You know why." He'd told her plenty of times that the whole idea of small-boat sailing is to harness the wind, disturbing neither water nor air. The way Jojo and Charley

30

had taught him, a motor on a small boat was almost immoral.

"It's dumb," she grumbled.

"Come aft," he said, trying to calm her. "It's hard to sail with your weight on the bow. Besides, I think the wind's changing. It comes around sometimes with the turn of the tide."

"What does that mean?"

"We'll have to beat home, that's all."

"That's all!" her voice slipped up an octave. "You said it was an easy run. What time is it?" She rubbed her shoulders. The sun threw shadows of the trees over the water. The boom slapped up and down. "Daddy'll hit the fan!"

He tried to make light of it. "Why would he do that? Get his hand all messed up."

"You idiot! You don't know what he's like when he's mad. He nearly killed a little dog once that snapped at Jamie. Pulled out his belt and beat him so hard I thought he'd break in half."

"Tell you what," Paul tried again. "I'll tell him this swordfish got ahold of the anchor and dragged us halfway to Block Island. We were going to cut him loose but thought about all those dinners he'd make. We could even stop at the market and pick up a few slices to make him believe it."

Then her anger really burst out of her. She stood facing him, hands on her hips. "You'd joke your way out of anything. Like telling Danny he was privileged to hit somebody like you the day you crossed his bow. Yesterday you pivoted us around the mark, pushing off the buoy, knowing we'd be disqualified. 'That's so much fun, let's do it again,' you said. What kind of teacher are you? We're supposed to learn how to sail right, not—"

"We're moving again," he said softly. "Better sit down."

Then he added, "Being becalmed is part of sailing too."

"We're not getting anywhere," she sobbed. "Mom will think we've drowned. And I'm starved. Did that ever occur to you?" She picked up the floorboard and smacked the water. "At least you ought to have a real paddle."

"I did, but Danny borrowed it last week after the bucket fight." Her body looked like one tight knot. "Your dad won't beat you or anything, will he?" He was thinking about that dog.

She was quiet a long time. Just the slap of the boom, the slosh of the awkward board in the water, her tense breathing. "So here we are, up the creek without a paddle." He couldn't see in the dusk whether or not there was a smile left in her. He knew she was scared, not of the dark or the water, but of getting home late.

She began to speak again, softly at first, listing his sins. He didn't try any more jokes.

"You didn't bring enough food for lunch and dinner. You should have known the wind would die. You should have known the Greenwich tide would take us up harbor instead of out. Why did you lend our only paddle? Why did you mess up my life?"

The last words caught them both off guard.

He stared at her wet face, the accusation in her eyes. He couldn't leave it like that. He groped. "We'll be okay," he began. "There's no danger of drowning or blowing out to sea. No danger of being robbed or mugged or hit by lightning. A little hungry maybe, but you're shivering and shaking over what might happen to you when you get home, instead of looking at the most incredible sky I've ever seen. Did they have sunsets like this in Texas?"

She looked. There were just enough low clouds to set up a panorama of pink and gray and purple, reflected in the glassy water. She brushed at her eyes. He saw her lower lip twitch, then soften. "But everything's changed," she said.

32

He went on, hoping his voice would calm her. "That sky is an old man lying on a gray corduroy bedspread, tired after a long day, pale around the edges from all the work he's done in the field, but peaceful too. You can see how easy and relaxed he fits the old corduroy. He's wearing his faded pink shirt; his arms are folded on his chest, and his beard is a white wool scarf across his neck."

"You should be a writer."

"I'll think about it. Thanks for the idea."

They watched the tired old beautiful man grow sleepier and sleepier. She got over being mad, admitted she was scared. She admitted the calm sea wasn't Paul's fault. As the light finally died—the old man shut his eyes and went sound asleep, they decided—it was so beautiful she put down the makeshift paddle and sat beside Paul in the stern. She leaned against him, and he held her shoulder to keep her warm. They watched him fade away.

You always made me see things differently, Paul. Sometimes being with you was like lying on my bed with my head hanging down. Fun, but scary. I couldn't stop the way you changed me, even though I was afraid and you made me mad. I've never seen anything or any person the same way since I met you. I'll never forget how the water looked that night, or the way you talked about it.

Your voice could shift so fast from teaching to teasing to serious to something almost soft and young like Jamie, some feeling in your voice that could bring tears to my eyes. I couldn't keep up with you. I'd be trying to figure what I was supposed to learn, and you'd be laughing at me for taking so long to get a joke.

Whatever happened then, and after that night, whatever happens to us today or tomorrow—maybe just a swim at

Matinicock Point, maybe more—you gave me that way of seeing. Nobody can take it away.

Darkness closed in while they were still east of the rocks. A nice steady wind came up, but with it a thick, rolling fog. Paul headed out to avoid the rocky point between Greenwich and home. It extended way offshore, and most of the rocks were submerged. One sharp peak could puncture the hull even in a light wind. He didn't know how far out to go. He listened for a bell, for another boat. He heard only the sibilant whish of water in the centerboard well, the creak of the rudder. He peered into the mist like a blind man until his eyeballs stung.

"What do you think your folks will do? I was sure we'd be home long before dark. Even running lights wouldn't help in this soup." He couldn't summon his usual light tone.

"Maybe it'll be okay," she said in a small voice. She was trying to comfort *him*. "I mean, I don't know what they'll do. I never stayed out late before. It's different for you. You're older. Nobody cares what you do or when you come home." She stopped suddenly, as if she'd heard what she said.

"It's true," he said as lightly as he could. "I'm the best yardman they can find." He felt the warmth of her shoulder, felt her shiver. He laughed. "Except for Charley. He'll be chomping his cheeks till the last of his boats are in."

She leaned harder. He kissed her then, the first real kiss. She didn't pull away. She shook. And when he stopped, she moved her lips to his and didn't pull back until he put his hand on her breast. Then he was scared too. (How long was it since he'd touched someone? His mother had hugged him—clung to him—the night his father finally died; they knew they didn't have him to take care of together anymore.)

34

He took his hand off her breast, but he kept his arm around her shoulders. They didn't talk for a while. He realized she was crying.

Sometime later the fog lifted and the wind picked up. They saw the Big Dipper. He tightened the sheet and the mainsail filled. He steered toward what he hoped were the right lights on the distant shore. He heard a motor. His heart raced. He didn't know whether from her nearness or from fear.

"You're right," he said. "Everything is changed. Are you sorry?"

She didn't answer.

I'll never forget that kiss, my first with you or any boy. When you stopped, my lips felt cold. I wanted to go on and on. Then you asked if I was sorry. How could I answer? Sorry or glad or a thousand exploding stars in my chest—I didn't know what I thought or what I felt. I was so frightened when you touched my breast, I thought the worst had happened. When you took your hand away, I wanted it back again. I started to cry—I didn't know why— and was afraid you'd see, so I turned my head away. But I wanted you to kiss me again.

Suddenly the whole starry sky appeared. "Look," you said, "the Big Dipper. The North Star, Polaris, will show us the way home." I was okay again because we could talk about the stars and the constellations. You knew them all and all their stories. You told me how they changed in the different seasons. You showed me Cassiopeia and Lyra and the brightest star Vega. You promised to take me sailing again in September when Orion, the hunter, would appear. You told me the super-giant star Betelgeuse in his shoulder was as bright as Vega and red.

"Beetle juice!" I said.

"Juice to some and goose to others," you said. "It's from some Arabic word meaning shoulder or something. I always miss Orion in the summer, and Sirius, the dog star, which is right behind him and the brightest of all."

I asked how come you knew so much, and you told me astronomy was your best subject. You promised to take me to the planetarium sometime. I said I'd love to go. You told me how to steer by the stars.

When he finally sailed up to the dock, Cassiopeia was halfway up the sky and the Dipper lay on the horizon. He left Mary Lou with the gear, wearing both their shirts, shivering and hugging herself to keep warm, while he moored the boat and swam to shore. The cool water hit him like a shock. Just as he climbed on to the dock a Coast Guard boat came along.

"You kids from the sailing school race?" a man called from the deck.

"Yeah," Paul said. "We got 'calmed."

"Had a call out on you. Quite a few hours already. Where were you? How'd you slip by us?"

"Fog, I guess," Paul mumbled.

"You'd better get hopping. I'll phone to let them know you're in."

They walked down the center of the dark streets. He was dripping wet, jogging to warm himself. He could feel her fear.

He took her hand. "Listen, I'll stay by you, whatever happens. I'll tell them it was all my fault."

She didn't say anything, but she gripped his hand tight like a kid on a roller coaster.

"When we get to your house, I'll wait by the tree. Give

36

me a sign from the window. I won't leave till I see you're okay."

Her fingers dug into his palm. He thought about what her father might do. He couldn't imagine anything. He wondered what salty way Charley would tease him in the morning. He was due at the dock at eight to clean up the boats. He thought about that kiss and what it might mean. He thought about kissing her again. He thought he'd wait maybe a week and then call her folks and ask if he could come visit in the day. If she wanted him to. He thought about kissing her now, one more time before they got to her house.

He was unprepared for the scene when they came around the corner. All the lights were on. A police car, top lights twirling, was in front. Two cops were on the path. Mr. Siddons was in the open doorway yelling, yelling. Paul had never heard anyone yell like that.

Mary Lou dropped his hand. Her father came toward them like a bear, grabbed Mary Lou, and yanking her by the arm, dragged her up the path and threw her inside. He slammed the door so hard the bang filled the night.

The bear returned. Paul stood helpless, dumb. Someone gripped him from behind and turned him. Angry voices exploded in his ears, and there were hands all over him.

Lying on the hall floor, I could still hear him yell. I wanted to cry, "I'm not your daughter!" I wanted to scream. I couldn't do either. I lay on that vinyl listening to some crazy man raging. I didn't know what half those words meant. I had to tell myself over and over: That's my own father. I thought he was going to kill you.

Finally Mom helped me up. She felt peculiar—warm

and cold mixed up. She was always afraid of him—I knew that—but now I knew why she'd said so many times, "Don't upset your father." I'd seen him mad. I'd seen him "blow up." I'll never forget him beating that poor puppy. But still . . .

"Are you all right?" Mom kept asking. It wasn't until weeks later that I knew what she really meant.

I wasn't all right. I've never felt all right since. But I got upstairs somehow, Mom half-holding, half-pulling me up. While she turned down the bed, I looked out the window, but you weren't by the tree. The last I saw, you were bent facedown over the hood of the police car and they were searching you. I didn't think your bathing suit had any pockets. I was still wearing your shirt.

"Get to bed," Mom said. She pulled me away from the window. "We'll talk in the morning." She put out the light, and I was more alone than I'd ever been in my life.

FOUR

"Piled in kinda late, dincha, son?" Jojo greeted Paul in the kitchen the next morning.

"Um." He never felt he had to account to Jojo the way he had to his father. Jojo didn't usually press him.

"Better tell me about it." There was command in the old man's voice that surprised Paul.

"Why?"

"Phone calls last night. I caught one of them, but your mom got the other. Coast Guard out. Cops came by this morning. But those calls—"

"What about them?" After what he'd been through last night, Paul didn't need this kind of inquisition from Jojo.

"In my day nobody talked like that, leastways not to a lady or a stranger on the phone. What'd you do to get the man so riled? What kind of trashy people are these?"

"Stop!" Paul exploded. "I didn't do anything to her or him either. And she isn't trashy. Forget it, Jojo. Just forget the whole thing."

Jojo scratched his forehead over his left eyebrow the way he did when he was figuring out something.

Paul poured himself a glass of milk.

"I can't do that, Paul. It's not usually nothing that makes a boy keep a girl out till three A.M. Or makes a sane man lose control."

"He's not sane. He's crazy."

Jojo's eyebrows went up. "He's the girl's father. She's mighty young. You better tell me about it."

"We got calmed, that's all. Couldn't get in."

"That all?"

Paul began to burn. Jojo didn't believe him. "We paddled about seven miles with a floorboard. When the wind came up, it brought fog, so I had to head out."

"I don't suppose you bothered to put running lights on board, or a radio so you could call for help."

"A radio? In a Blue Jay? Anyway, we weren't in any trouble. Just late."

"You were in trouble," Jojo said quietly.

"It was dumb about the lights, but we meant to be back way before dark." He didn't mind Jojo's criticisms about the boat. "No lights," Paul went on. "No paddle, and no motor of course." Paul returned Jojo's dry stare. "No supper, no beer, no booze, no grass, no blanket, no sex." He stamped out of the kitchen, leaving Jojo scratching his head.

Sometime later he called the Siddons house and asked for Mary Lou. He hung up in the middle of the tirade that stung his ears. He felt hot to think of Mom hearing stuff like that. And Mary Lou. Was her father always so crude?

Paul fiddled around his room trying to think. He should be at the dock, but he didn't feel like facing Charley yet. Mr. Siddons' voice had made him feel dirty. He ran his hands over his thighs. He took a shower, letting the hard points of hot water pummel him, numbing him. He thought about what life could be if people would just leave people alone.

He needed to talk to Mary Lou. He wanted to hear her laugh, say it was okay, say "Oh!" He didn't know how he was ever going to see her again.

Three weeks till school started. Once he helped Charley

pull up the boats, the summer job was over. What would he do for three weeks? He couldn't stand any more of Jojo's questions. He could imagine what his mother was going to say.

Paul dressed and walked the mile to the shore. He found Charley bent over the transom of one of the boats, screwing on the gudgeon, the rudder fitting. When Paul stood near, Charley looked up, squinting into the sun; his mouth was a straight line. His gray eyes were steady, clear, and as cold as the Sound in January.

Paul stuck his hands in his pockets. "Sorry I'm late, Charley. What d'you want me to do?"

"Nothing." The answer came fast. Charley looked back at the gudgeon. Paul went home.

In the attic he found his sleeping bag, and it gave him ideas. He rummaged through his elegant grandmother's old Vuitton trunk. In it he found a dented canteen, his father's army belt with big grommets and brass hooks. He put it on, remembering how he used to dress up and play soldier when he was little. He took off the belt. He was past games.

At the bottom of the trunk he found an old L. L. Bean catalog, his Swiss army knife, a long-ago birthday present from his father. They used to read the catalog together, planning trips, planning all the equipment they'd like to buy. Paul thought about the big trip, his coming-of-age present. Mom and Dad had vacationed in Colorado once before Paul was born. Dad loved the Rockies and always meant to go back. It seemed he spent half his life planning trips he never took.

Paul found a couple of Bean's protein "Energy" bars that had been in his Christmas stocking the year Dad died. He could have used those last night. He wondered if they were still good, or if in five years vitamins and proteins disappeared like dreams. He pocketed the bars.

He went through the catalog page by page, not seeing

41

the pictures or reading, not seeing anything but the cold distance in Charley's eyes, like the endless reach of water on a gray, windless day. The word "nothing" seemed to bore into Paul, filling his mind and body until he was as hollow as the word.

Finally he closed the trunk, closing in the army uniform, his father's fishing gear, photographs, his childhood. But he took with him the sleeping bag, the wide webbed belt, the canteen, and the mess kit.

He heard his mother come home. Her voice mingled with Jojo's. He waited in his room until she called him to dinner. He felt feverish. As soon as he sat down, the questions began.

The girl, the police, where they'd been so late, that man, those obscenities! "You had a girl but you never brought her home. Why?" Her voice filled the kitchen, bouncing off the white surfaces. He was watching a movie. The sound track was going.

"I've never heard language like that in my life," she accused him, as if Paul had said those things.

"Now you have." He hated this character he played. He was in the movie now. "You'll get over it. I'm going away." He hadn't known he'd say that.

"Where are you going?" Jojo asked.

"I don't have to tell you." He flinched at his mother's indrawn breath. He never talked to Jojo like that, but his throat was so tight and his chest hurt so that words pushed out of him he didn't mean, or that he meant but didn't mean to say.

"Don't make sense to rush off without knowing where you're headed, boy," Jojo said. "Stick around. If what Mr. Siddons said wasn't true, then how will you prove it if you walk away?"

"If!" Paul bellowed. "Whadya mean if? That cinches it. You two don't trust me either!"

He stamped upstairs, grabbed the sleeping bag. He remembered to get his toilet kit too. And the half-written letter to Mary Lou. And an old pair of sneakers in case his boots got wet. And an extra shirt and pair of jeans. And his camera. He was nearly out the door when he thought of his bankbook. He rolled all the stuff up in a towel and shoved it into the middle of the sleeping bag. He hooked on the army belt and clipped the folding knife onto one of the hooks. By the time he went downstairs again, he'd cooled a bit.

He found Jojo leaning on the mantel, scratching his head. Little puffs of smoke rose from his pipe. His long gray face looked longer and grayer than ever. Suddenly Paul wondered how old Jojo really was. Surely over seventy, but he always joked about his age. When his hip joints hurt, he'd say he was ninety-nine that morning, and would Paul please take out the garbage. When he felt like going for a sail, he'd say for a fifty-fifth birthday present how about a turn around the red nun. But he was old enough so he didn't single-hand the Ensign anymore. And he'd take out a Blue Jay alone only if somebody else was sailing nearby.

Mom sat in the wing chair in tears. She hadn't cried when Dad died.

"I'm off," Paul said.

"Oh, Paul, no one in our family ever had trouble with police."

"Don't worry about it," he said. "I didn't break any laws. I'm going to New Hampshire till school starts. It'll blow over by then."

"Who with?" she asked wiping her eyes. He saw relief on her face. She wouldn't have to look at him. He'd do her a favor by leaving.

It was hard to breathe. Why was he angry at Mom? She hadn't done anything. He was angry at her and wanted to protect her too. Nothing, he felt, made any sense.

"Billy Cobbs and I have a deal. We're going to climb

Mount Monadnock. Always meant to do that." (With Dad, he almost said. They never mentioned Dad.)

"Billy Cobbs? Do I know him?"

"He's been in my class for years." Liar. The name just flipped into Paul's head when he needed a name in a hurry.

"Do you know the way, Paul? You're always so sure you know the way."

"I'll take a map."

"But how will you get there? We can't let you have the car. Does Billy drive?"

"By bus."

"Do you have any money? Call me every day."

"Yeah. No. I mean, I've got money and no, I won't call you every day. There aren't any phones on a mountain."

"Every week then."

"I'll call sometimes," he said.

The morning after, I wouldn't get out of bed. Or you might say I couldn't get out of bed. Or I suppose my mother might have said I needed the sleep so I shouldn't get out of bed. At any rate, I slept and pretended to sleep on and off. Sometimes pretending, sometimes sleeping. I went over and over everything about our day. Half-knowing I wouldn't see you again, I tried to memorize every second. With the pillow on my head, I replayed the swim, that kiss—how it made me feel—the fog, the stars, that beautiful old man. But whenever I came home and heard my father, sleep overwhelmed me like a blanket. Sleep—my only way to hide.

Since then I read somewhere that people who are sick in their minds sleep a lot.

Since then I've read a lot of things.

You can't imagine what it was like. Every time I woke

44

up, if I heard footsteps in the hall I'd bury my head under the pillow again. Eventually he'd have to go to work, I told myself. I had a bad taste in my mouth, but I wouldn't get up. I heard their voices in the hall. I heard the phone ring, but when he answered, I buried my head again. I knew you'd call if you could. I tried to imagine where you were, what the police had done to you. But I wouldn't get up. I wouldn't ask.

FIVE

Paul spent the night in a half-built house in the middle of a swamp they called the Frogs. It was a well-known hiding place for couples, gangs, kids, and fugitives. One year a girl was raped, her boyfriend killed. Now there were only two reasons anyone would come here—to hide or to do something illegal. Paul came to think.

He found a stash in a coffee can near where he spread his sleeping bag. He rolled one, lit, and inhaled. He waited for mind pictures, peace. He'd smoked on and off since seventh grade, never steadily. Never if he needed his wits. He could take it or leave it. Tonight he wanted to take it, but nothing happened. He smoked till the last bit burned his lip. Maybe like people, energy bars, vitamins, and dreams, the potency of pot diminished with time. Maybe it never was any good.

He didn't sleep. He lay passively studying the two-by-fours over his head, the kicked-in place on one wall, the obscenities in pink spray paint on another. He shuddered. Like himself, he thought, this place had been used and abused by strangers. Graffiti wouldn't wash off any more than the shower had made him feel clean.

His life reeled out like film before his eyes as he tried to figure out why he was here, what he was going to do, and whom he could talk to.

One thing was sure: he wouldn't stay in town doing nothing for three weeks, not with Mr. Siddons on a rampage, maybe even sending the police after him again. But where to go—the only place he could think of was west. He was sixteen. Dad would approve.

What about Mom? She wouldn't approve anything he did. He closed his eyes, trying to blot out the way she'd looked. He half-wanted to go home and comfort her, tell her he wasn't bad, tell her he'd do anything she said if she'd only stop crying. But he hurt; she should have believed him without any explaining.

He hadn't talked to her in a long time. Whatever he said invited criticism. Phrases burned in him: *You used to be so responsible. What's happening to you?* Nothing. Nothing was happening. He was grown-up and tired of being told how nice he used to be.

For a long time he hadn't known anyone he could talk to until that day he saw Mary Lou in her red shorts on the dock. Now Charley wouldn't look at him; Jojo and Mom condemned him. Dad was dead, and he couldn't even talk to Mary Lou on the phone.

Alternately perspiring and shivering, Paul slapped at the mosquitoes that whined about his head. His mind reeled on. The frog chorus roared. His head ached and his chest pounded. Anything could happen to him here. It would serve him—all of them—right if he didn't survive, if he disappeared. As the first gray light slipped into the skeleton structure, Paul pulled his sleeping bag over his head as if to postpone dawn. He hid not only from the light but also from the all-too-vivid memory of that final hour.

He'd been a damn fool to sail to Greenwich instead of finishing the race. It'd been a crazy impulse, a lark. But it wasn't criminal. In the sweaty darkness of his sleeping bag he remembered the kiss, swimming to shore, and then . . .

One iron hand pressed his forehead on the hot metal

hood of the police car; another clamped his wrists behind his back, hurting them; others pulled at his bathing suit and probed. He writhed under the hands and the voices.

"*This the boy, sir?*"

"*That's the motherfucker.*"

"*Shall we hold him?*"

"*Damn right. Hold him. Jail him. Get him outta my sight or I'll kill him.*"

"*You'll have to bring charges. We can't hold him unless you bring charges.*"

"*What?*"

"*He's clean.*"

"*Hold the bastard!*"

"*Do you want your daughter examined for rape, sir?*"

Paul left town after ten that morning, but he wasn't "clean." He had what was left of the stash in one pocket and his last eighty dollars from emptying out his savings account in another. He headed west, not north, and not by bus but by thumb. He had three weeks to find the continental divide and get home again. The Rocky Mountains beckoned and threatened him.

His first ride was with a kid about his own age who drove a beat-up Mustang. "Where you headed?" he asked.

"Colorado."

"For good?"

"No. Just a break. A party."

"Cool," the kid said. "Then what?"

"Got to be home in three weeks."

"Why?"

"School starts."

The kid was silent a minute, then said, "That was a big waste of time for me. I quit after the ninth grade. Been working ever since." He sounded proud.

"I only have one year to go," Paul said. "My mom'd

48

have a fit if I didn't finish. Everyone in our family studies a lot."

"Whatcha going to do with the paper they hand you? Frame it?"

Paul laughed. "I don't know. Sell it maybe. If you work all that hard, it must be worth something."

The boy didn't answer, just pressed his foot on the gas pedal. Paul watched the factories slide by, the miles clock down on the parkway. The farther west he got, the freer he felt, the looser the bands around his chest, the lighter the pain in his throat, the easier it was to breathe.

The next ride was with a shoe salesman from Altoona who drove a '77 Pontiac, one of those long deals, all hood and no leg room but lots of power, the kind of car Jojo would have called a living room. Paul never expected that car to stop. Well-dressed middle-aged men usually sped by like the women, as if they were afraid to stop.

Of course they were afraid to stop. Being afraid of hitching or picking up hitchers wasn't anything he wanted to think about. The Pontiac zoomed by. Paul had already turned to look for another car when he heard the horn. Crazy bastard was backing up right along the shoulder of the parkway. Lucky there wasn't much traffic.

Paul jogged to the car.

"Hop in," the man said.

Paul threw his gear in the back and climbed in, heart beating. Every time he got in a car that wasn't driven by a kid, his heart whanged away. Scary. Kids, you trust. Older people, you never know. There was no reason to be scared, it turned out.

"Where're you headed?" Usual question. But checking the gray hair, half-rimmed glasses, coat and tie hanging on the hook by his shoulder, Paul knew not to be flip.

"Colorado."

"What's in Colorado?"

"Home," Paul lied. "I had a summer job for my uncle in New Jersey. Got to be in Denver before school starts."

The man grinned. "Good boy. Glad to hear it. What do you study?"

Paul shrugged. "Anything, I guess. I'm still in high school."

"I mean what do you like? History? Math? I used to love math. Used to be like a game to me. Probably could have gone on with it, too. I should have gone to college. You headed for college, son?"

"You sound like my dad."

"How so?"

He was a history freak. Always reading some thick falling-apart book about the old Norsemen. But he made his living doing something else."

"I sell shoes. What did he do?"

"He had a job in New York."

"I thought you lived in Colorado. Your father lived in New York?"

"We moved."

"Who did he work for in New York?"

"Some big construction firm. He was an engineer. He didn't talk about it much."

"What did he talk about?"

"Oh, everything else, I guess." Even as Paul told this stranger about his father, he knew he wasn't saying the right things. How do you tell what someone talked about five years before? How do you tell how different your house sounds without him? It was a relief to talk about him, though. He told the man things he'd never told anyone, not even Mary Lou.

How he'd wait, doing his homework every night until he heard the door open downstairs, heard the clump, clump as Dad stomped the snow or leaves off his feet, heard the closet door open, shut, the murmur of his mom's voice,

50

"That you, Harry?" from the kitchen. Though Paul was named after his father, Harold Paul Bachman, they used his middle name to keep from mixing them up.

"It wouldn't matter now, would it?" Paul said. "Now I could go ahead and use the Harry or Harold, because you can't get mixed up with somebody dead."

"That's right, son," the man from Altoona said softly.

Harry would come upstairs, stop in the doorway of Paul's room, and ask, "How's it going?" Sometimes Paul thought about his father as Harry. A real person, not just a father. Harry.

"Okay," Paul always answered. Then he'd follow Harry downstairs and sit on the hassock at his feet. All the words of the day would come rushing out: what some teacher said; the math problem he couldn't do; where he went after school; some tricky piece of boat hardware he needed. Paul would go on and on, his father grunting now and then or saying, "I'll have a look at it later," until his mother would appear with a drink.

"Paul," she'd say, "let your father breathe. You haven't stopped talking since he got home."

Most of their dinner conversation went over Paul's head. But if there were a book in the mail, Harry'd light up. He'd say, "If the new project goes, maybe I'll take a year off and study. I could still get a degree. You don't make much in the academic world, but you get long vacations. I'd chuck all this tomorrow if . . ."

"Why don't you?" Mom would say. "We'll get by. I'll work full time."

"I'm too old. I should have done it twenty years ago. Drop it." He'd even get mad at her.

"Suddenly he was tired all the time," Paul told the man from Altoona. "He'd fall asleep in the middle of a sentence. 'It's the damn commuting that's killing me. Next year I'll ask for a local office.'

51

" 'Next year may be too late,' Mom told him. She was right about that. One night he fainted in a restaurant. He couldn't breathe. They did a lot of tests in the hospital, then sent him home. Cancer was eating his lungs away.

"Six months later he was dead," Paul finished.

"Too bad," the salesman said.

The green signs went by—Stroudsburg, Berwick, Bloomsburg—and they crossed the wide Susquehanna. Paul noted the miles that grew between him and the ache he'd left behind. Route 80 seemed an endless stripe through dark green hills, past pleasant farms and dark slag mountains, scarred hillsides of deserted strip mines.

Altoona said, "I have to head south at Mt. Eagle. Do you want me to drop you at the Loch Haven exit?"

Paul studied the map. "Which is the best way west?" he asked.

"Depends what you want to see. There's a lot of country to cross before you see any mountains."

Paul said, "Anywhere I can get another ride is okay."

They rode in silence awhile. Suddenly the man said, "Kid, how come you're running away?"

"I'm not."

"Your home isn't in Colorado any more than mine is. Never was. Listen, I don't know whether anything you've told me is true, but I'm sure of one thing. Somebody'll be lying awake nights worrying about you."

Paul was silent.

"Want to know why I picked you up?"

"Why?"

"You looked like my kid. Same hair. Fooled me for a moment, so I backed up for you."

Paul's hand touched his head, coarse straw to his earlobes.

"Yeah," Altoona was saying, "you look like him, not the way he was last time I saw him, but the way he used to be."

52

"How's that?"

"I don't know where he is now. That's how that is."

Paul didn't know what to say. He hadn't thought about Altoona being a real person, having a wife and kids. Just a thing, anonymous, someone to talk to while he rode west. Not living, hurting, or feeling.

"What happened to him?" Paul asked finally.

"Don't know. That's the point. Nothing happened."

"I don't get it."

"There's nothing to get. Nothing happened. Nothing. One day he was an ordinary boy, late for school, hotshot on the basketball court, no big cheese. Just a good kid, mowing lawns, staying out too late, beering it up weekends like I used to. We were talking about college. We visited a couple—U. of P., Penn State. One day he said, 'So long, Pop, I'll see you,' and moves in with a girl of twenty-eight who does dope. Last time I saw Bobby, his head was shaved and his clothes were all rips and safety pins." Altoona passed a truck full of chickens, needle just about 75. "He wanted a handout."

"You give it to him?" Paul asked.

"Hell no."

"Then what?"

"Then nothing. Nothing. No word for eight years. I figure I've wasted twenty-eight on him."

"Maybe he's okay," Paul said. "Just mad for not getting the handout. He'll come back when he doesn't have to ask for anything."

"After eight years?" Altoona tightened his lips. Then he said, "Have your fling, kid. Climb a mountain. Screw a girl. But don't do dope. And go home, kid. *Go home.*"

He pulled into the exit, drove to the stop sign at the intersection, grinned at Paul, and waited for him to get his sleeping bag from the back.

"Good luck," he said.

"Thanks. And thanks for the ride." Paul slammed the

door. "Okay," he said to the back of the Pontiac, "of course I'll go home. What kind of a chunk of wood do you take me for? I'm on vacation. Loose. Free. No hassle for three weeks. Great." He hoisted the pack to his shoulder and looked around to see where he was. Nearby was a Shell station with what looked like a lunch place next to it. He was halfway across Pennsylvania and he'd been on the road seven hours. Not bad. He'd grab a bite, pee, and see if he could get into Ohio before night.

He picked up a couple of road maps and bought a Baby Ruth, which reminded him of Mary Lou. He went to the men's room. He was sitting on the pot when he noticed the paper crudely taped to the inside of the door. He started to read it, stopped, finished on the toilet, and then, more as an afterthought than anything else, took the paper off the door. At the counter he ordered thirty-five cents' worth of french fries and a glass of milk. He reached for the ketchup. He read the paper. There was a map and a drawing of some stick people in a circle holding hands around a globe. The margins were decorated with leaves and flowers, and a sun was drawn at the top. The headings were carefully hand-lettered, but most of the message was typed.

THAT THE SUN WILL SHINE
Sunshine Family Tribal Gathering for International Peace

Howdy! In the sincere belief that ALL PEOPLE *of the earth* CAN *live in perfect peace, harmony, and love, we will once more meet at* SUNSHINE FALLS *for three days of perfect harmony. Join us in that great green meadow that God provided where we will gracefully share our know-how so we can work together to make this a garden planet where all creatures can live in harmony and freedom,*

nourished by the bounty of the earth. Councils
will be held as well as health, education, music,
and art meetings. Bring what you can, including
your long green, which we are ever in need of.
This gathering is absolutely free.

There was more, but the waitress brought the fries. He ate them dipped in ketchup, drank the milk, paid, and walked out to the crossroad. He stuffed the paper in his pocket and stood in the afternoon sun at the point of intersection with the access road to Interstate 80. He raised his thumb.

How many good rides would he need to get where he was going? *Where was he going?*

I think now that everything about you is different. You didn't have heavy thighs before. You have a new scar on your heel. Your fingernails are ragged. You used to be full of fun and now you're almost brooding. You're avoiding looking at me—no, you're checking the luff on the main. I can't believe I remember so much that you taught me. Remember when you let me ram that boat? I was excited when you asked me to go sailing. But here we are, and we can't talk. I like talking to you in my head—I've always carried on imaginary conversations with people—but we can't just sail in silence all day. I want to know everything about you. I want to tell you . . . well, some things.

The absolutely worst thing that morning was that I was so hungry. When I finally got up after Daddy left, Mom made me some scrambled eggs. I wanted to turn them down, but I was starved. I ate every crumb, and two pieces of toast.

She said, "I'm glad you're eating so well, dear. That's a

55

good sign." I wouldn't say anything back. I was mad at her too, though I knew she couldn't help what Daddy did. I remember the poppies printed on her dress and the bacon-and-Ivory-soap smell she always had. I remember thinking it would be a big relief to just put my head on that dress and cry. I couldn't. I was afraid to let her see anything I felt, because if I showed even a little, then everything would show.

I stayed in my room all afternoon. I listened for the phone, sure you'd call. I tried to write you a letter: Dear Paul, Are you all right? . . . Dear Paul, I'm so ashamed. . . . I doodled and ruined at least six sheets of good paper. Finally I straightened out my underwear drawer. Dumb.

My father'd said I mustn't leave the house. I felt like a prisoner. I refused to leave my room even for dinner. I heard him say, "I earn the money. I expect my daughter to greet me. Is there no discipline in this house?" I could imagine Jamie's big eyes, Mom trying to simmer Daddy down.

To make it easier for her, I decided to go downstairs; but I made a decision. I wouldn't talk. I put this look on my face, even practiced it in front of the mirror. It said nothing could touch me. I'd do what he said, but I wouldn't let him see how I felt. It was like wrapping myself in foil. That way I could keep my feelings about you secret and unspoiled. It was pretty romantic. I decided I really was in love with you and my father had ruined my life. I'd be as sad and passionate as Cathy in Wuthering Heights. I've always liked sad books.

The absolutely worst thing was getting through dinner, starting with the blessing. I felt as if I was lying to God. I wasn't thankful to anyone for anything. And when Daddy started his lecture, about my reputation, all that stuff about drugs and fast boys, those stupid ugly phrases made me cringe. What he said didn't have anything to do with you and me. When he told me I couldn't go anywhere without

him or Mom for a month, I nearly broke down, but I raced
to my room before I burst into tears. It was as if my insides
were spilling all over my bed. That's the only time I cried.

The absolutely worst thing was I missed you. Sad books
are one thing, but it's no fun being sad. I couldn't call you.
I wanted to hear one of your terrible jokes. I wouldn't
mind one now, but you're not in a joking mood.

I wonder if you'd still like me if you knew everything
about me, if you knew what I was thinking, that right now
I'd really like to go up on the foredeck and have a smoke.
I didn't do those things two years ago. I'm not the same
as I was.

SIX

Squinting into the sun, Paul shifted his weight and stretched his legs. He checked the billows in the main where the jib backwinded it, let the sheet slip through his fingers till the sail was taut. He glanced at the telltale and the masthead fly. Wherever he looked, Mary Lou was in his vision. Wherever his mind roamed—past, present, or future—she was there too. He caught her watching him.

"What woke you?" he asked.

"I wasn't asleep."

His eyebrows went up. "You sure gave a good imitation."

"I was thinking."

"So you learned to think while I was away," he teased.

She studied her hand.

"I was thinking it was nice to be out here again, remembering what you taught me."

"So you do remember. That's a plus."

"Everything," she said. "That doesn't mean I can do things right, but I remember everything." She looked straight at him. "Not only about sailing."

It was uncanny. He'd almost said that too.

She went on. "I was thinking that everything we do and say makes me remember, makes me wonder about things."

"That's right," he said softly. "I know. I'm remembering things too."

"You're not mad at me anymore." She eyed him carefully.

"I never was."

"You sure gave a good imitation."

"Not at you," he amended. Then he frowned. "I'm sorry. Since I got back, I can't seem to do anything right. Even with you." He was saying more than he wanted, but he had to be fair with her. "There are certain questions, like who I am or what am I going to do that—"

"Or where are we going?" She was almost teasing.

"I thought it would be different," he said. "Maybe easy, the way it used to be."

"Maybe it is," she said.

He didn't know what she meant. Not true—he did know. She was ready for him, ready to talk and to listen. She was burning to find out everything about him.

She said, "Last week you were nothing. You didn't exist except as something that happened to me way back when I was a little girl."

"That's it." He laughed out loud. "That's what's so different. You've lost your Texas accent!"

They heard a shout, "Starboard!" Paul looked under the genny and saw a huge sail too close, and the white hull of a Soling ahead. They were on a sure collision course.

He rammed the tiller across, yelling, "Hard alee!" and uncleated the jib sheet. The sail flew out over the water.

Mary Lou fell off the seat. "Trim the jib!" he cried while he pulled in the main as hard as he could. The huge loose sail cracked as the wind caught it. She scrambled to grab the flying line. Just as the boom slammed over, barely missing her head, the boat heeled suddenly to port. He leaned over to help her pull in the sheet. The jib wouldn't come around.

"Winch it," he said, but the sail was stuck on the forestay. "Go up and free it," he begged. "Fend us off if you have to." The flapping sail made a terrible racket. Mary Lou clambered onto the deck and tugged at the sail. The hull of the Soling loomed. Mary Lou reached high on the steel cable. Paul tended the tiller, whispering to himself.

Suddenly the genny broke loose and whipped around. He almost dropped the tiller trying to haul in the sheet fast, hand over hand.

"Fend us off!" he yelled. Mary Lou was poised, one hand on the stay, one slim leg extended over the water as the distance between their prow and the sleek white boat shrank.

With less than a foot of water between them, the bow of the Ensign finally swung around. The wind filled the sails; the other boat headed off, and they slid silently by without touching.

"Damn you, I'm racing," the man cursed into Paul's ear.

He barely looked up as he mumbled, "Sorry."

Mary Lou gingerly made her way back to the cockpit. "I'm all bruised," she said, rubbing her shoulder.

"Sorry," Paul said again. His voice shook. She took the jib sheet from him. "Better not cleat it till we're clear of the race. We'll have to come about again in a minute, and maneuver through the rest of the boats."

"They are gorgeous," she said, catching her breath.

There might have been twenty other Solings sailing parallel, all heeled at the same angle, their sleek hulls gracefully curved, low in the water, slicing through the waves toward them.

"Best-looking boat ever made. Be ready to let off the jib." He liked having her beside him again, but they were tense, hearts beating hard. Beautiful or not, that encounter with the lead Soling had been too close. He felt stupid; he hoped the man hadn't lost his lead.

She said, "I never handled a genoa jib before. It's a monster. It comes so far back, and I couldn't pull it in. I guess I was too weak."

He was surprised. "Hey, that wasn't your fault. I'm the one who ran us straight into the Solings' starting line."

"Does the genny often get caught like that?"

"No—it really was my fault. I got caught not looking and let off the jib sheet before I had the other end. Dumb thing to do."

Suddenly she laughed. "You won't make that mistake twice."

"Turn the line around the winch again," he said. "It does all the work. Ready about?" He measured the distance to the next boat. She looped the loose sheet from the starboard side twice around the winch, ready to grab.

"Don't let go till the bow comes all the way across the wind; when the wind gets on the other side of the sail, let her off fast and haul in like mad on the other side so the jib doesn't have a chance to get loose. That last come-about was so lousy. My timing is off. Damn fool place to be." He was almost talking to himself, and his hands were shaking, his vision blurred.

"I never was that good," Mary Lou said, trying to make him feel better. He saw her hands were shaking too. He tightened his grip on the tiller. How rusty was he?

"Couldn't we use the small jib?" She sounded scared.

"Not in this light wind. The boat won't sail right. Don't worry." He tried to sound confident, but remembered how often he used to say that to her. As much to convince himself as her, he said, "We'll get better as the day goes on. We'll have plenty of practice getting past this race. Ready?" His vision had cleared.

They came about again, and nothing went wrong. They smiled at each other, crossing to the high side together, shoulder to shoulder again, legs touching.

"You were great," he said.

"I'm glad you aren't mad at me anymore."

"I told you. It wasn't you. It was me. Ready about?"

They tacked back and forth until they were out of the

61

Soling race. They got better and better. Another race was about to start.

Suddenly Paul yelled, "Hey, look! There come the S-Boats. There's number twenty-two! That's Charley! I used to crew for him."

"Sailing-school Charley?"

"Sure. Hey, Charley!" Paul yelled and waved, but the boat was upwind and his voice didn't carry. He was excited. "The Ensigns ought to be out soon. There's the committee boat, and the Y.R.A. buoy."

"What's Y.R.A.?"

"Long Island Yacht Racing Association."

"I forgot."

"The starting line is between their buoy and the committee boat, see?" He felt the way he used to with her, teaching, sharing his excitement. "The Solings were first— they're a new design, sleek and fast. Couldn't exist without fiberglass. Tall mast, narrow mainsail, big jib. Now the S-Boats are lining up. They're maybe a sixty-year-old wooden boat, Herreshoff design, haven't been built in years, but look how well they're kept. The Rhodes Nineteens will be last, because they sail a shorter course. With this wind they'll use the mid-Sound birdcage off Rye for the first leg, then the red bell off Scotch Caps for the downwind spinnaker leg."

"You like to race," she said. "I thought you hated it."

"I don't know," he said. "I think I used to like it before . . ."

"Before you met me? Your never used to want to race when we were out."

He grinned at her, touched her cheek with his fingertip. "I guess I had other things on my mind," he said.

She licked her lips. She didn't mind him touching her. The way she looked at him, he knew she didn't mind at all. Suddenly he wasn't sure how he felt about that. He sheeted in the main a bit.

"Would you want to race again?" she asked.

"You mean now? Today?"

He didn't answer. He stared at the S-Boats, then shifted his gaze to the Solings, now far up the Sound, an uneven row of receding tall triangles. Suddenly a bright orange spinnaker ballooned into the air.

"Must be first around the mark," he said, again feeling that lift of excitement, that tense poised moment before the huge light sail went up, before the wind caught and lifted it high in front of a boat. Then a blue spinnaker appeared, then a red. "Let's sail closer and watch them," he said.

"They're pretty." Mary Lou sounded excited too.

"I don't know about racing," he said. "If you do it, you can't do anything else. You spend all your time messing with the boat, sanding the bottom, fixing the rigging. All your money, all your time, all your thoughts have to go to the one thing. To make your boat, which is just like every other boat in that race, perform a little better. Everything matters. Even a barnacle on the hull can slow you down, maybe just enough to be passed by the boat that's smoother. The rake of the mast, the set and condition of the sails—"

"The rake?" she asked.

"That's how far it's tilted either forward or aft. Given the same wind," he went on, "the same water, the same boat design, what makes one go faster than another?"

"I thought it was how good a sailor you were."

He nodded. "That too, of course. How you read the water, where the puffs are, when to tack. The guys who are out here every day don't care about anything else. You should hear them curse at their crew when a line comes loose or a spinnaker doesn't go up right. It's so easy to make a costly mistake. Sometimes the crew is the guy's wife or kid. They get so mad. But they have to work like a team to win. I never wanted to race when you and I were out because I wouldn't have been with you at all. To win, I'd have needed crew I wasn't distracted by and could get mad at. Winning a race just isn't that important to me. I don't think it ever was."

"What is?" She almost whispered the question, as if she was afraid to stop him.

He wasn't sure how to answer. Finally he said, "Oh, living well, I guess. I don't mean being rich or having a lot of things. Having a good time is important. Liking what you do. Not being angry at anyone. Being good at something but not worrying about it so much you forget to see things or enjoy your friends."

She laughed then. "Sounds great to me." She stretched her feet across to the other seat. "I sure would like to be able to do what I want to do forever. Not to have to do anything."

"What do you have to do?" he asked.

"Mostly boring things. Go to school. Study a lot of boring things like math and English. I love to read, but I hate memorizing all that stupid vocabulary. And Spanish. Ugh."

"When I was in school, I never minded it that much."

"It's a hassle," she said. "People are always at you. Do this. Do that. If you miss one little test, they mark you down. What's happened to your grades, Mary Lou?" She imitated a teacher's tone. "Have you cleaned your room? Done your math? Turn that stereo down. It's always something."

"You sound like me before I went away."

"There's a boy who wanted me to go to California with him in his van."

Paul was startled. Of course—she was sixteen now. She went out. "And?" he said.

"It wasn't much fun just staying home. Lots of my friends traveled or went to camp. I thought about it but . . ."

"Let the winged fancy roam. Pleasure never is at home."
Again, words in his head slipped off his tongue.

"What?"

"Friend of mine used to say that," he explained.

64

"A girl?" She sounded jealous. "Did you go sailing with her?"

"No. I never sailed. Not like this. Not with anyone." He wished he hadn't mentioned Amy.

"But you were in California, weren't you?"

"For a while," he said, wondering how she knew.

"What was it like?" she asked him suddenly. "What was it like not having to do anything for anybody? Just to go where you wanted, and when. What was it like being so free?"

He didn't know how to answer, so it was a long time before he spoke. Finally he said, "I had to do some things." He knew she wanted more than that, but he wasn't ready. Can a person cut out a piece of his life, like two whole years, he wondered, snip it out and live from then on as if it never happened? Did he *want* to erase those years? Again he felt panic, almost as strong as when he thought they'd ram the Soling. Past and present were equally terrifying. Future unknown. He was here, home where he'd chosen to be, and with Mary Lou. What was he afraid of? It was easier to talk about sailing.

"Ready about?"

They tacked again and he pointed to the shoreline. "There's the bell off the point. We'll pass it, then reach into the bay. It's deep to about thirty yards offshore, so we can anchor in close; the beach is nice."

As they approached, the shore gradually became defined. Paul could pick out houses on the hilltop, and the white sandy edge to the water. He was getting hot. He was ready for a swim.

I like you best when you talk about sailing. You get caught up in it, excited the way Jamie is when I take him to the zoo. And you know so much. You can still turn a conversation, though. One minute I think you're going to kiss me, and the next minute you've gone somewhere I'm not invited. I wish you'd tell me more about that girl. Sort of. I know I'll be jealous.

I wish you'd tell me about her so I could tell you about Roy. And Barb and Danny. And so many things. I don't know about Roy. He doesn't really mean anything to me, but I wonder what you'd think. Would you be jealous?

You don't have any right to be. You weren't around. That awful first week at home I listened for the phone all the time. By Friday I knew you wouldn't call. By the end of the second week I stopped looking for mail. I didn't find out from Jamie until nearly Thanksgiving that my mother stole a letter from you. By the end of the third week I told Jamie not to bother asking around about you. By the time school started I half-wondered if you'd been real. Maybe I only dreamed being kissed in Greenwich harbor. Then I decided you were real enough, but you hadn't really liked me. Then I decided to be a tragic heroine again. It was love, and my father had driven you away. Round and round. By the time I got back to school I felt I'd been let out of a dark cellar.

You know how it's blinding at first when you come out of the dark into sunlight? School seemed like that. So noisy. Girls jabbering about what they'd done and boys they'd been out with, books they'd read, movies they'd seen. I didn't say anything to anyone. The only movies I'd seen were old ones on TV. Danny and a couple of the other kids from sailing class said hi.

I wondered how a tenth-grader could get to talk to a senior. I watched for you in the halls, on the lunch line, and on the steps in front of school. I tried to remember what courses you said you were going to take.

On the way to lunch a neat girl named Barb—I'd hardly known her the year before—said, "Hi, Tex." I'd hated that name when I first came. I thought they were making fun of me. But that day it sounded friendly. She said, "Where were you all summer?" I realized I wasn't a new girl anymore. I was accepted.

"Right here," I said. Danny was in the line too. He actually winked at me.

Barb laughed. "You're blushing. Hey, what did happen to you this summer? Danny, what are you not telling?"

Barb and I went to nearly all the same classes, except she took French instead of Spanish; we walked home together. I found out she lives in the next block. She got to be my best friend. She's the first person besides you I ever talked to here.

Barb had been away all summer, junior counseling at a camp for handicapped children where her little sister, Mimi, goes. Mimi isn't very handicapped; you can't see that there's anything wrong. Barb told me she's brain-damaged and can't do some things the way other people can. She's a little uncoordinated, so she's happier in a special school. The camp sounded great. Barb said it made her feel so good to be able to work with little kids and be able to help them. The way she described it, I thought I'd like to do that too. I love her sister, Mimi.

Barb also told me about her boyfriend there, how far they'd gone, and that she didn't like immature people.

I told her how you and I always ended up in the same boat. That's a funny way of thinking about it. We were then, and we are now. I don't know about in between. I wonder if I ever will. I wonder who that girl you knew is who doesn't like her home.

SEVEN

It had been raining the day he met Amy. He'd gotten west of Omaha, slept in a corn crib by the roadside. He'd been on the thumb for three days. Rocky Shores was suddenly too remote. He wondered what Mary Lou was doing. As far as he could see, the land was flat and brown. He was somewhere in mid-continent, adrift, too far from safe markers. He'd rushed off for the great divide like some wounded animal looking for . . . What? He hit his forehead with the heel of his hand. His father. Who was dead. No matter how tall and beautiful those Rocky Mountains were, Dad wouldn't be there.

He got off the highway and sat among some coarse-leafed bushes. It started to rain, lightly at first, then harder. He'd seen a sign for a town called Wahoo. He studied his map, which was getting wet. It didn't show any mountains, but there was a river and some green place called a recreation area. He was tired of cornfields, flatlands, and straight roads. He yearned for a curve, a river, a hill. New Hampshire was all green with lakes and hills.

The rain was wind-driven now. He gathered himself up and jogged to a gray wooden building with a Coke sign, a lunch place where he'd sit out the rain.

Three hours later he was still staring at the brown roses on the wallpaper and at the rain. He wondered what artist would be so gloomy as to paint brown roses, when a wet girl came in. She had long black wet hair, big dark eyes, full lips, and not much chin. She was small and her T-shirt was glued to her skin so he could see her breasts right through, pretty big for such a little girl with no stomach and no hips.

She sat at the counter and ordered two cups of coffee. She drank first from one cup, then the other, so they'd cool equally, Paul guessed. Water dripped from her rump down the edge of her seat onto the floor. She carefully dried a book she'd been carrying and began to read. After a while Paul realized that not all the water was from the rain. She was crying. So after another while he went to sit beside her. He looked at the book. Poetry.

They got talking. It turned out she and her boyfriend had been on their way to a Hindu religious retreat in Colorado that was supposed to be an earthly paradise. But in Omaha they'd had a fight. He'd left her without saying just where the paradise was. The last she saw of him, he was getting on a bus with a ticket he'd bought with the last of their money. She decided to keep going. If she found the paradise, she wouldn't need any money, because the whole deal was you gave up all your worldly goods anyway.

"Must be rough to be left alone," Paul said, suddenly feeling guilty about leaving Mary Lou. "How long had you been together?"

"Oh, not long." She kind of threw the words away, and wiped her wet face with a paper napkin. She'd been in the middle of her sophomore year at Hofstra, she told Paul. "All my life, I was supposed to be a teacher, so I was taking all these education courses. Suddenly I realized I didn't understand most of what I was supposed to learn, and I didn't want to be a teacher, because most of what I'd learned in school was nonsense. So what would I tell the kids?"

She and some friends in the dorm figured screw it, and got stoned every night. That semester the only course she passed with more than a D was English, because they were reading poetry. The teacher assigned some Keats, and that turned her on. She and her boyfriend decided Hofstra wasn't where it's at. He told her about this paradise in Colorado. But in Omaha he said they couldn't take grass into the paradise. She said she didn't think that sounded very free, and they had a fight.

"Being with him wasn't so great," she told Paul. "You know, the chemistry." Paul nodded as if he really knew. He wondered how many guys she'd "been with" so she could compare.

Suddenly she pressed her book against her chest and looked straight at Paul. "I'm glad he left. He wasn't much. I don't need him or his paradise. Just somebody nice around, grass when I want it, someone to talk to. How far do you figure Colorado is, anyway? Listen." She didn't wait for Paul to answer, *"Ever let the fancy roam. Pleasure never is at home! At a touch sweet Pleasure melteth. Like to bubbles when rain pelteth; Then let winged Fancy wander/ Through the thought still spread beyond her. . . ."*

His mind wandered. It was like music, her voice going in the background, singsong. He still had seventy-five dollars. He'd been careful. Didn't eat much. He wondered if he could make it to Denver in one more day. Maybe two. He thought about traveling with Amy. It wouldn't be so lonely.

She stopped reading. "You have a joint?"

He told her about the stash he'd found, but that it might not be any good.

"No matter. I'll try anything."

He reached in his pocket and felt the piece of paper there. "Hey, look." He spread it on the counter between them. He hadn't finished reading it. Now he did. And he read the ending out loud.

70

*We are simply brothers and sisters bound
together by our love for each other and by our
desire to live in peace. We hope this gathering
will be an example of Paradise. Amid the
cathedral of Nature we'll work together for the
benefit of our beloved planet Home.*

PERMIT TO GATHER TOGETHER
Congress shall make no law respecting an
establishment of religion or prohibiting the free
exercise thereof . . . or the right of the people
peaceably to assemble.
   —From the First Amendment to
   the Constitution of the United States.

A FREEDOM AIN'T A FREEDOM UNLESS THE PEOPLE
ARE ALLOWED TO EXERCISE IT.
   —The Sunshine Family

Paul studied the map, pointing it out to Amy. "This
looks like Paradise is a lot closer than Colorado. It's probably only fifty or a hundred miles from where we are right
now."

Amy put her head down on the counter. "I'm tired,"
she said, "and I don't have any money."

She looked as if she needed taking care of. Paul felt the
pad of bills in his pocket. He liked the sound of three
things: sunshine, family, and peace. Three things that were
missing from his life.

"I've got a little," he said. "Are you game?"

She shrugged. "Okay. If you know the way."

The phrase hit his brain like a shock. *"Do you know the
way, Paul? You're always so sure . . ."*

"Hey, I gotta make a phone call," he said.

"Who to?" Amy asked as if she'd known him all his
life.

"My mom. I promised to call her sometimes. I forgot."

"Be careful," Amy said.

That was a weird thing to say. "Careful?" he asked.

She nodded, then read, "*Quickly break her prison-string, and such joys as these she'll bring . . .*"

He shook his head. She sure wasn't any Mary Lou; he could get tired of all that poetry. "You're crazy," he said. "My mom's okay. She just likes to know where I am, since my father died."

"I thought that once too," Amy said, "till the day I called mine and said I was quitting school. She melted the wires."

"But I'm not quitting school," Paul said.

Amy shrugged and opened her book.

Paul held the old-fashioned receiver, a black horn with a thickened end, against his ear and listened to the ringing. His mother answered. That was good.

His lips touched the black mouthpiece. "Hullo. How's it going?"

"Paul! Where are you?"

"I just thought I'd call. Like I promised."

Her voice came through shrill. "Paul, you lied to me." She sounded very upset.

"For Crissake, I haven't even said anything yet. How could I have lied?"

"I tried all week to find you. I've been so worried. You disappeared. Then yesterday I called around town to find Billy Cobb's mother."

Paul felt he'd been kicked in the chest.

"Paul, I thought maybe she'd heard from *her* son."

Paul held the receiver away from his ear, looked at it. But he could still hear her voice. "There isn't any Billy Cobbs, is there? . . . Paul?"

"Well . . ." He tried to think of something easy.

72

"First the police, then that dreadful man, now I discover you've lied. What other lies have you told me?"

She sounded like the baby rabbit he'd once found, its belly ripped open by a cat, shrieking in spits and spurts. It had shrieked and cried until it died.

"None, I guess. I dunno." He was six again; he'd messed Joe's papers.

"You guess! You don't know. How can I believe anything you say?"

Paul felt as if somebody was inside his chest, scraping everything away, hollowing him out. Lies and truth, he thought vaguely, those words had no meaning. You kept life even; you said what people wanted to hear. The only lies that were lies were the lies you told yourself. The only truth that was true was the inner truth of knowing who you were and where you were going. But if you didn't know where you were going, did that mean you lied? If you made up something to make somebody you loved feel better, something to say so she wouldn't worry . . .

"You can't, I guess," he said eventually.

"Where are you?" the wounded rabbit cried again.

"In Colorado." That wasn't really a lie. He was headed there. Some quick instinct made him not say Omaha or even Nebraska. She sounded hysterical. Thoughts of her calling the police went through his head, even though she'd never done anything like that. But she'd never caught him in a lie before, either.

"Colorado! Not even New Hampshire. What are you doing?"

"Oh, looking around." He glanced at Amy, deep in her book, her black hair dry now, soft and waving around her puffy cheeks.

"I want you home, Paul. There's so much to do here."

"I'll be home by the time school starts."

"I suppose I can believe that too."

73

"Well . . ."

"Come home now."

"In about two weeks." She was silent. He could hear someone in the room.

Then the old cracky voice was in his ear. "Ayeh?"

"Jojo, listen," Paul said, "Mom sounds upset, really awful. Calm her down, okay? I'm fine. Nothing's going to happen. Tell her it's okay, will you?"

"In my day," he heard the old recording, "a fella didn't just walk out on his responsibilities. If he got in trouble, he stayed and faced it. If someone got in trouble in my family, they'd have a meeting, talk it out, give him his criticisms, and he'd thank them for it."

Paul took a deep breath. "Jojo, I didn't walk out. I'm on vacation. Tell her. For God's sake, Jojo, can't a person have a vacation?"

He heard his mother's voice again, in control now but crisp and careful. "I have only one thing to say, Paul. . . . Paul? Are you there?"

"Uh-huh."

"Come home now. Today."

"Mom, I can't."

"Fly. Have you money? I'll send—"

"I'll get home later." He looked at Amy. *Sunshine, peace, and paradise.* "Sometime before—"

"Today, Paul, that's final."

He looked at the receiver, a disk of black plastic with seven little holes in it. It wasn't his mother—no flesh, no body from which he had been born. It had no connection to him. Just a horn of plastic with some holes and some scratchy sounds coming out. Not even a dying rabbit. Nothing that could hurt him. Nothing he could hurt. Nothing much to bother about. He hung it up.

Back at the table, Amy studied his face. "I warned you," she said.

It took me nearly a month to believe you weren't in town. Barb found out from someone that your mother didn't even know where you were. Then I got mad at my father all over again. I never dared call your mother. I figured she was probably miserable enough.

At least I had a friend. I still missed you, but I could talk to Barb about it. One day she asked me if I was in love with you. At school the girls were always talking about being in love. I said I didn't know. When you were here, everything I felt was too new and confusing. Now that you were gone, the whole summer seemed unreal.

She said, "You may have strict parents, but I don't think you're immature." The worst thing Barb ever said about anyone was that he or she was immature.

I didn't feel so out of things at school anymore, even though I wasn't allowed to go out. Barb said dating was silly. Boys and girls should be friends and not worry about who asks who out. I told her my father would never let me phone a boy. "Girls wait. Boys call," he told me over and over.

"He's stuck in the last century," Barb said.

I never told her what he'd done to you. I was too ashamed. Someone who pretends to have all those high standards, to talk like that, to accuse somebody without even trying to find out the truth. I know those words now; it doesn't bother me when my friends use them. But they don't go around yelling them or telling other people what to do.

Once I had a feeling he even might be ashamed himself. He bought me a new dress—he'd never done that—just came home with it under his arm. It was off-white muslin with embroidery around the hem. Pretty. I thought he was trying to bribe me. The dress hung in my closet a long time before I ever wore it.

One day in November when the leaves were blowing all over town, Danny Elbe—we called him Elbow because he managed to get to the front of every line—walked home with Barb and me. He and Barb had begun going together, though she swore she wasn't in love with him. Halfway home he offered me a joint. I didn't know what to say. I'd heard plenty about them, and read enough, but I'd actually never seen one.

I wanted to take it, to smoke and survive just to show Daddy that he didn't know anything. A lot of kids I knew had done dope for years. I didn't want to admit I'd never tried. And I was scared, too. Finally I said, "I don't feel like it now, Danny." He didn't make a deal over it. Just said "Bye now," when they dropped me at my house.

I called Barb later that night. I said, "You don't smoke pot, do you?" She took so long to answer that I knew she did. But she was great. She got good marks and took care of Mimi a lot, and had a job three afternoons a week doing ironing for a neighbor. She was pretty and had a good figure and could go out as much as she wanted, so long as she was home by midnight.

"Does it hurt?" I asked her. "My dad says it'll make you sick, maybe die young. Does it?"

"Gosh, no!" Barb laughed. "It's just fun. A hayride. Just don't do the hard stuff."

I thought of the things my father said happened to kids. I thought of how he thought I'd already done it with you, Paul, and how he made the police search you. I wished I'd said yes to Danny.

That was the night Jamie told me there'd been a letter from you that had been mailed from Arkansas. Mom had looked at it a long time, he said, and put it in her pocket.

The next time Danny asked me, though I still was scared,

I said yes. We went down behind the clubhouse and sat looking over the water. The Sound was gray and gloomy, not shining the way it is today. That smoke was a big disappointment. Inhaling hurt my throat, and nothing happened.

Danny said, "Don't worry. We'll try again. You didn't learn to sail in a day either, did you? Barb and I need a little time to teach you."

I realized he and Barb talked about you and me. Danny and Barb and I became a threesome after that. They kept me in books, pot, and laughs. It was so easy to be with them. Mom and Daddy never minded if I spent the night at Barb's. They knew her parents from church.

When it got cold, Daddy started talking about trying to get transferred back to Texas. I decided that if they did, I wouldn't go.

I wonder what you and that girl you mentioned did together. I wonder what it's like in California.

EIGHT

Paul and Mary Lou were past the point before they spoke again, and then only because he asked her to let off on the jib.

"Sure," she said, and slid to the low side to uncleat it.

He watched for rocks, scanning the bay. He didn't want any other surprises. He also watched her. Just seeing her was like the first cool swallow of a good can of beer, feeling the cold dry fizz all the way down.

August days are iffy—sometimes scorching calm, sometimes broken by sudden storms that can blow up from any direction. This day, wind and sun were kind, as if blessing their new time together.

His memory surprised him. He seemed to have forgotten nothing about handling a boat. Or Mary Lou. He hadn't figured out all the ways she was different. It was more than just losing the child part of her, that scared daredevil he'd known. She was certainly more womanly, prettier, less gullible. But there was an underlying restlessness, even a sadness that bothered him. He wasn't sure he wanted to know what caused it.

He'd slipped mentioning Amy. He was afraid of Mary Lou's curiosity. He wished he'd stuck to the business of sailing—"Trim the jib . . . ready about." But he couldn't stop looking at her, the way she crossed her ankles, licked her lips, squinted and tossed her hair. He wondered if she ever braided it. He thought of taking off the rubber band, knowing it felt like silk, corn silk, long enough to braid.

He wished she didn't know a boy with a van who wanted her to go to California.

Helplessly he said, "Do you ever braid your hair?"

Startled, she answered, "Sometimes. It's not really thick enough. Why?"

"I'd like to watch you. I knew someone who did that."

She blushed. He was relieved. He'd been testing her.

"The one who quotes poetry?" she asked.

"No. Not that one."

"But she's pretty."

"She was. She looked a little like you. For a minute I was afraid you might be like her. You're not. Ellie never blushed."

"Ellie," she repeated.

He stretched his legs and scanned the white crescent of sand. They were headed straight to shore. Ellie had never been sad; nothing ever made her blush. All experience passed through her without affecting her, he thought. He would have liked to tell Mary Lou more about her, but it was too soon.

"I never found out where you'd gone," Mary Lou said. "I tried. No one knew. I wanted to write you." He noted that she was still careful about questions.

"You didn't get my letter."

"No. I found out you wrote a long time after. My mother stole it."

"It was probably a stupid letter," he said. "You know, I tried to phone."

"More than once?"

"No. Once was enough."

She blushed again. "I figured." He knew they were thinking about the same thing.

79

He watched her long fingers play with the end of the jib sheet, unknotting it, knotting it, twisting it around her finger, leaving the figure-eight knot in the end, finally tossing it down.

When she spoke, it wasn't as if she was making excuses or even talking to him. She was thinking out loud, and he happened to be there. He didn't mind. The Sunshine Family acted like that too. He was used to it. Anyone said anything that came into his head, even if it didn't have anything to do with anything. At first he'd thought it crazy, but later he did it too.

"My father used to blow up when I was a little girl. I hated it, but got used to it. He never yelled or talked like that when there was company. Mom explained his temper to me, telling me how a man feels about his only daughter, as if she's some kind of princess. I think—I thought—that's dumb. I never could look straight at Daddy after what he did to you. And I never forgave him."

Paul didn't know what to say. She looked at him straight. He saw the plea, the apology, everything, in her eyes. Serious eyes. Not teasing him now, or daring. Not the wide child eyes he remembered, either. A woman's eyes, begging him to trust her, asking the questions she didn't dare voice: *Where did you go? What did you do? What have you done without me?*

He wasn't ready to answer, but he was liking her. "I think you tried to tell me that once, when I was teasing you about being afraid to be late. I'm sorry I didn't listen better."

"You don't have to be sorry," she said. "You didn't hurt me. He did."

Paul squinted up at the masthead fly, ducked to look under the jib again. He wasn't sure she was right.

"Hey, how about going forward, watch for rocks. When we're a neat swim off, I'll come into the wind and we'll drop anchor. I could use a swim before lunch."

"You brought lunch." She laughed, tossing her hair. "That's a switch. I thought we'd starve again. What is it?"

"Hobo three-green salad and pita," he said. "Mother Nature's own. I fixed it myself. I dare you to eat it." He didn't tell her he had dinner on board too. He'd see how lunch went first. He almost laughed out loud at himself. Two meals ahead. He had actually planned that far.

On the foredeck, she checked the anchor and made the line fast to the mooring cleat. Pleased that he hadn't had to remind her, he thought maybe he could make a living teaching fourteen-year-old girls to sail, even run a sailing school. Then he mocked the thought. He'd lost two jobs the week he'd come back because he couldn't remember what he was supposed to do. Who'd trust their daughter with you, dumb-ass? he asked himself. Dropout. Derelict. Addle-brain. Good for a carwash vacuum expert. Sailor? Hell no. Fair weather is no test. So you got through the races all right after nearly bashing only one boat. Any idiot can sail in a breeze like this. His hand shook again when he reached over to uncleat the jib. He let it off, then loosened the main, holding the two sheets in one hand.

He called his plan to her, not daring to trust dropping anchor to memory—hers or his. "Wait for the boat to stop, then drop the anchor and as soon as it's caught, let down the jib. I'll get the main."

"Okay," she called. She stood on the deck, held the fore-stay in one hand, the anchor in the other. He could see the sandy bottom, maybe six feet down. The tide would pull the boat back, dig the anchor in easy. The maneuver went according to plan.

Don't get cocky, he told himself as he furled the sail and made the lines fast. Can't be more than eight knots of wind in this bay, and no waves. Anyone who's had two sailing lessons can do what you're doing. His hand was shaking again. He knew what he wanted, and knew he didn't want it either.

No. He'd come this far and might need to go a lot farther. He wanted to control his mind, not addle it. He stead-
ied his right hand with his left. Nobody knows where you
are, he said to himself, except you and Mary Lou. He
straightened up.

"All set?" he asked, grinning at her.

"I guess." She stepped out of her shorts, revealing the
bikini layer.

He was startled at how her figure had changed, no child
now. Her breasts, such small points before, were full. Her
waist was narrow, widening slowly to rounded hips of a
larger woman. But unlike the woman he'd known, there
was no extra flesh, no softness or plumpness.

His grin widened. "Sure don't waste a lot of money on
bathing-suit material, do you?"

She stared him down. "The less there is, the more they
cost." Then she dived in, a brown shining fish with two
orange stripes. She was beautiful. But she'd never had
smart comebacks like that before, he thought.

He dived after her, felt the cool water like a drug soothe
his senses. He rolled over and over before he broke the
surface. He ducked under again, gargling the brine, down
and up, swimming hard now, hard crawl with plenty of
splash, now coasting, arms to his sides, just absorbing the
cool, the salt taste. He felt alive everywhere.

He swam to the boat, climbed in, and watched Mary
Lou floating peacefully on her back a few yards off the
bow. He stared with some admitted hunger at the long
smooth expanse of tanned belly between the orange stripes.
He got the basket out of the cuddy, took the lunch bundle
and a six-pack of beer from the cooler.

Holding the lunch in one hand over his head, he let
himself over the side carefully. He swam to her. "You take
the beer. I'll get this stuff onshore dry."

They swam together to the white sand and pebble beach.

They planted the beer behind a rock underwater. They took two cans up the beach, found a high and dry rock with a wide ledge where they could eat. Paul popped his can, took a long slug, felt its fizz hit his stomach, then unwrapped the lunch. They were both so hungry the food disappeared fast.

"Now I know what you meant about living well," Mary Lou said, licking the remains of the salad off her fingers. "That was great. You sure learned how to cook."

"I had to. I like it, though," Paul said.

"What was in it? You must have spent hours dreaming it up."

"Anything fresh," he said. "Sprouts. Zukes. Celery. Cukes. Everything but meat."

"You don't eat meat?"

"Not if I can help it. Not that sandwich stuff."

"I had a friend who didn't eat meat. I thought he was crazy."

"He? The one with the van?"

She lifted her chin. "He," she said. She stared him down again. Eventually he studied the sand between his feet.

"I suppose you have a lot of boyfriends," he said.

She stood up suddenly, brushing the crumbs off her legs. She laughed and put her hands on her hips. "I go out," she said. "I suppose you never looked at a girl. The poetic one. Or the one with the braids."

He squinted up at her. "I looked," he said.

"I figured." She turned her back and walked toward the point.

"Wait." He gathered up the trash and stuffed it into one bag, careful not to let a paper fly. "I'll walk with you."

She ambled back. "You always were a good trash collector."

For a moment he was lost, then remembered the day he'd first met her mother. Laughing, he said, "I guess we never shake our old roles, even if we try. Once a garbage man . . ."

"But now you're a cook too," she said. "Here, I'll dump it for you. What about the beer?"

"Thanks." He handed her the bag. "It'll be all right. Tide's almost all the way in." He pointed to the line of seaweed at the last high-tide mark. "Let's walk."

They started toward the point. She said, "My mother makes a gross pudding out of apples and old rolls. Daddy loves it."

He took her hand. While they fooled around with the idea that old rolls were as stale as old roles, tossing it back and forth, he fooled around with her fingers. By the time they reached the boulders that formed the long breakwater protecting the bay, he had a firm hold and he led her, finding good footing, from rock to rock, until they were at the point. They sat watching the waves break on the rocks and eddy in pools between, wetting the snails and barnacles deep in the crevices.

He put his arm around her shoulders. She took the band off her hair. It blew across his face, but he didn't mind.

Suddenly he liked the differences he found in her. Daring translated became confidence. Experience wasn't necessarily good or bad, two sides of a coin. It happened. You were changed. No one should stay a child forever.

"Tell me about the boy with the van," he said.

"Tell me about the girl with the braids."

"She's dead."

"Oh!" And then, "Did you love her?"

"I'm not sure. I might have. But Ellie loved everyone."

He hadn't meant to say so much, but it was all right. Perhaps it would help to tell her about Ellie.

Mary Lou nudged a snail with her toe. It came loose and tumbled into the deep.

"Poor snail," he said. "He'll have to climb all the way up again. I wonder if he'll make it."

84

"He'll make it. He's healthy enough."

"But maybe he's down too deep," Paul said. "That's a long climb. Maybe the tide will change and he'll be washed offshore."

"Maybe he wants to go away. Maybe he was bored with living on this same rock forever. Maybe he wants to go somewhere else."

"The wind's changed," he said. "It's coming out of the west now, blowing toward Cold Spring Harbor. We could run up there. It's the most beautiful harbor on the Sound. Wouldn't take us more than an hour if the breeze holds."

"Is it going toward Greenwich too?" she asked.

He let go of her shoulder. "Yes."

"And will it die at sunset?"

"Probably."

"And will we starve again? And have to paddle home?"

"There's some dinner fixings on the boat. In case you get hungry." He held his breath. He didn't know what he hoped she'd say. Going away with her would be . . . well, it would be something. But this time, he thought, there would be no coming-home scene.

She pulled back her hair and put the rubber band on again. She licked her lips. He knew they tasted of salt.

Then she said, very slowly, "I told Mom I was spending the night at Barb's." He didn't know who Barb was. He didn't care. "So, if the wind did die, it wouldn't matter if we were becalmed. That just wouldn't matter at all. I think it would be wonderful to see the most beautiful harbor on Long Island Sound. Today."

For a long and terrifying moment they were all around him, slipping their arms into his, touching him. Ellie and Amy and Cat too. And they were all telling him different things.

"Well," Mary Lou challenged him. "What do *you* think?" And then again, "Well?"

He saw her suddenly, and the others disappeared. He

85

smiled and pulled her to her feet. "We'd better hurry. Catch the wind and tide while they're in our favor."

You go away and you come back and you go away and you come back. When you're away you frown as if you're sick and terrified. When you come back you're as good as I remember. It's awful about that girl dying. I wonder how. I guess you'll tell me sometime.

I should never have brought up Roy. Now I'll have to tell you something. I don't know what. I don't want to sound as if I'm bragging. I don't want to sound silly. I don't want to admit that I haven't been anywhere, done anything. Even to camp. I wanted to go with Barb last summer, but Daddy didn't think it was a good idea. A long, boring summer. If I hadn't met Roy . . .

I don't want to talk or think about Roy or Reggie or Danny. I want to think, pretend, or believe that you still love me. There, I said it, at least to myself. Through all the months and the dry-eyed nights, no matter what I did, I kept the way I felt about you locked up tight in a secret place where no one or nothing that happened could touch it.

But I don't want to make it too easy for you, either. I wish I could call Barb. She's not like me, but she knows me. She asks good questions. When Roy wanted me to do it with him, it was Barb who said, "Do it if you want to. There's no right and wrong. But, don't do it if you don't want to."

She and I agree about one thing. Girls who go all the way when they don't want to are immoral. Barb and I talk about that a lot. We agree that it's important to decide what's moral and immoral. The boys say anything, whatever they think up fast, about morality, because they want to go farther. Barb always told me, "Trust yourself to know." But I never did. I know I'm the only one I ought to trust, but I still don't. Even now.

I want to go away with you. Not just for now, or for tonight. But when Roy wanted me to go to California with him and I really wanted to, I didn't trust myself. So how do I know?

He'd call me from work—he's the cook in this hamburger place where I worked for a while—and he had a neat velvety voice. He'd say things into my ear about the way I looked or the way he thought I looked without my clothes on, and I'd be hot and blush just listening to him. So I'd make another date, thinking: I do love him. I'll do what he wants. This time I really will go all the way. But I couldn't imagine what it would be like. I wanted to know. I didn't want to know.

I met Roy when I lied about my age and got a job in that hamburger place. When my parents found out, I had to quit.

I had to cut the lettuce. He was the cook. He flipped the hamburgers really high. The second day I was there he said, "I'd really like to take you home and flip you."

I think I liked Roy because I knew Daddy would hate him. It was sort of revenge. And Roy made me laugh. I found that out a while back—I like sad books, but I don't like being sad. I can't think of anything I'd like more than to sail to Cold Spring Harbor and walk on some beach with you forever.

NINE

"Are we lost?" Amy asked Paul. Their last ride had dropped them at a dirt road, a dusty chalk line that they'd walked along for hours, getting hotter and dirtier, getting nowhere, it seemed.

Paul dropped his sleeping bag, rotated his shoulders to loosen them, and took out the map again. "I don't think so," he said. "Let's keep going awhile. Maybe we'll get another ride."

"Here?" Amy waved at the woods and the untamed fields to either side of them. She took off her shoes and rubbed the arches of her feet. Then she stood up and said, "Oh, well, being lost is only relative."

"How do you mean?"

"Well, in order to be lost, you have to want to be somewhere you're not getting to. Since neither of us is sure where we want to be, or whether or not we want to be where we said we were going, or where that is, it's hard to figure that if we don't get there we'll be lost. We'll just be somewhere else instead."

Paul laughed. "In my whole life, I never met anybody like you. You're wonderful."

"Or nowhere," Amy said, and started walking barefoot. The dusty road with its scrubby green strip in the center was lined with brambles and trees. At one point the trees got taller, the brambles denser. They heard running water. Suddenly the road dipped and went through a small creek. Amy sat on a rock, planted her feet on the bottom, and wouldn't move.

"Come on." Paul tugged at her elbow. "Now I know we're on the right track. There's a creek on the map."

"I'll stay here," Amy said. "I like it." She opened her book.

"But I know we're close to the meeting place," Paul argued.

"This is good enough for me," Amy countered. "I'm tired of walking. The important thing to remember is that wherever you are, or are not, and whatever you feel like doing, or not doing, that's where it's at."

Paul crossed the creek and sat on the bank. He didn't know what to do, whether to leave her there or try to drag her along. He rejected the last as impractical. He tried to sort out what she was saying. *Wherever you are, or are not, and whatever you feel like doing, or not doing, is where it's at.* Hadn't he sailed to Greenwich with Mary Lou because he felt like it? Everything you do has consequences, Mom would say. And he'd be angry. Now, like somebody's mother, or Jojo, he decided Amy ought to move. But she stuck to the middle of a creek because her feet hurt. There weren't any laws to say she shouldn't.

Could you live a life of not caring where you were going so if you didn't get there it didn't matter?

Suddenly Amy stood up and joined Paul. "I'm smoothed down now," she said. "Let's leg it."

He helped her up the steep bank. Once beyond the noise of the rushing water, they heard a strange and different sound—vaguely musical, rhythmic, percussive, but too discordant to pass for music.

"I told you we were close," Paul said.

They emerged from the woods at the edge of a broad

89

unmowed field. Patches of orange and yellow wildflowers decorated the green. Paul shifted his pack to his shoulder. He could see an old windmill, a half-broken-down shed, a tent in the shape of a tepee. At the far end of the field, unexpectedly, was an old school bus.

It was almost unrecognizable. Paint of a dozen colors had been smeared over it in no pattern or design. He could see some wide brush strokes, drips, splashes, scribbles, and symbols. In some places the paint had been thrown.

Nearby maybe two dozen people milled around, some by themselves, some in groups. Smoke from two open fires rose into the still late-afternoon air.

As Paul and Amy got closer, they began to identify the music, such as it was. It had the monotonous beat of early hard rock. Amy began to move to it, faster and faster, shaking her shoulders. She walked on her toes. The beat seemed to pour into her. She began to run. Turning once to wave, she disappeared into a crowd.

A couple of boys played guitars. A man with a trumpet played out of tune and rhythm. A woman sat on the hood of the bus clapping two hubcaps together like cymbals. Another girl danced while she struck a piece of a muffler with a gearshift stick. Some band. Half the instruments were old automobile parts. No one payed the slightest attention to Paul. He wondered where Amy was.

Food smells came his way. He wandered toward one of the fires and saw an iron pot full of beans, but it smelled of a thousand other things. On the other fire was a washtub with some kind of stew.

A pile of raw vegetables lay on the ground, squashes, corn, onions, tomatoes. A hand-painted sign said, "PICK YOUR OWN APPLES—TREE BY NORTH FENCE IS RIPE AND READY." There was a bucket with what looked like pudding or mayonnaise near a heap of odd loaves of bread, rolls, some wrapped, some obviously hand-baked.

No one talked much—some people sang more or less to the drummer's beat, but not the same words. People ate with their hands. Those without cups or mugs dipped bread or raw vegetables into the beans or stew or the bucket of glop. The more Paul watched, the hungrier he got. He finally found Amy with a hunk of bread in her hand dipping into the bean pot. She looked happy. He thought, she'd never be lost in any crowd. Wherever she found herself, she'd make her place, home. Except Hofstra.

Home. He was hundreds of miles away, completely disconnected. He tried to conjure up Rocky Shores in his mind. He couldn't imagine being there now. Wasn't that what he'd wanted? But he wasn't connected to this scene either. He shrugged. No matter. He hadn't been searching for anything really. Just an adventure, a breather, time to let the atmosphere back home cool.

He strolled over to a man sitting on the steps of the bus. He was shirtless, and his long bony-kneed legs stuck out of cut-off jeans. He was bearded and his dark hair fell to his shoulders, but there wasn't much on top. Black brows dominated his thin face. He beckoned to Paul.

"Peace," the man said, holding up his hand palm forward.

"Hi," Paul said. "I saw your notice." He pulled the paper from his pocket.

The man nodded. "We welcome anyone who wants to share our grain, our love, our brother- and sisterhood, who wants to join us in rediscovering Mother Nature."

"I . . . uh . . . I haven't thought about it much," Paul said. "I just thought I'd see what it was all about. I happened to be going by on my way . . ."

That sounded silly. He tried again. "Actually, I was on my way to Colorado when it started to rain. So I figured I'd stop to see what your festival was like before I went on west. Is this all it is?"

The man scanned the field. "It's been better attended in

other years," he said. "Back in seventy-six we had close to six thousand brothers and sisters who worshiped with us."

"Wow," Paul said, not knowing whether or not to believe him.

"And of course, most of them have gone on home. This is the tail end, a few stragglers. Tomorrow we'll just be family again."

Paul nodded.

"But you're welcome in any case, though I'm afraid we're going in opposite directions. We've just come from Colorado. We'll head south in a few days. We follow the sun. By the middle of September we'll be in Arkansas, and Colorado will be turning all shades of red and yellow. Nights will be cold."

"I hadn't thought about that." Paul paused. The food smells were making him dizzy. "What would it cost for me to eat and spend a couple of nights here with you?"

"There's no charge. We're not running an American Dream motel here. What you see and smell is the bounty of the earth, given freely by the Mother for those who care for her, bless her, feed her, and in return cherish the fruits of her soil. The people you see are Mother Nature's guests—our guests. We always have arms open for the lonely, the homeless, those disenchanted with the computerized society that is desecrating and polluting the earth. You're quite welcome to stay as long as you like. I'm Sid."

"Well, thanks," Paul said. "I'm Paul."

Sid pointed to a heavy-shouldered man a few yards away, half-asleep leaning against the wheel of the bus. Clumps of brown hair fell across his forehead; his bib overalls looked three sizes too big. "That's Abe. He's the man you want to see about sustenance. Have you got your own tepee?"

Paul shook his head.

"You can sleep under the bus tonight. Might rain. If it gets crowded, try the apple tree. Those leaves give a fair amount of shelter."

He looked Paul up and down. "I see you have a sleeping bag. Good."

"And a mess kit, some cooking stuff," Paul said.

"Fine. That's a start. How are you on the long green?"

"The what?"

"Bucks. Bills. Wampum. Even out here, money is sometimes necessary."

"I have a little." Paul was taken aback. Hadn't Sid just said there was no charge? He didn't want to admit to the seventy dollars in his pocket. He'd need that to move on, he thought, and to get home.

"Good," Sid said. "Anything helps. Work it out with Abe. Any questions that come up, ask me or him. He'll introduce you to the Family."

"Oh! I just remembered. I'm not . . . there's somebody else."

"You're not alone? Well, few of us are. Not for long, anyway. Where is she?"

"I'm not sure. Last I saw, she was dipping into your beans."

Sid laughed. "Fine. Don't worry about it."

"I'm not." Paul laughed too.

He surveyed the scene again. It reminded him of a painting by Brueghel he'd seen in a museum his mother had taken him to, a huge painting filled with tiny fat people all doing different things, all in some kind of motion; like these people, though close together, they seemed not to notice each other.

A big blob of a girl with blowsy hair held her head with her two hands as if trying to keep it on straight. Elbows out, she danced and swayed, twirling, kicking her great-thighed legs high. A few men and women watched her, clapping to keep the rhythm, chanting, "Hi, Johanna; ho, Johanna; let the east wind blow, Johanna."

A very old, very bald man who could have been an Iowa farmer sat sipping out of a paper cup, nodding his head in time with the clapping.

Perched in the apple tree, a girl with long yellow braids tossed apples to three boys below. Some they caught, some fell; sometimes the boys fell too, apples bouncing around them.

The man with the trumpet climbed to the roof of the bus and tooted as if he were a rooster wakening the world.

A man and a woman lay on the ground holding each other, lips to lips, hips to hips, toes to toes.

It was a movie set, crazy and fun. Everyone seemed happy.

For the first time in Paul's memory there were no weights on his shoulders. He stretched them back, dropping his sleeping bag by the bus. He turned his face to the sun and closed his eyes. His self-consciousness dissolved. No one here knew him. Not even Amy. No one here knew where he had come from or what he had done. No one here would expect anything of him but whatever he felt like offering. He almost leaped with joy.

Instead he strolled the length of the crazy bus to the man called Abe. He was dozing. Paul decided not to disturb this peaceful creature with the broad soft face of an overgrown infant. He'd help himself to something to eat as Amy had done.

He felt a hand slip into the crook of his elbow. A female voice said, "You look hungry."

A small brown-haired woman smiled up at him. Her face wasn't pretty, but it had nice lines, sharp cheekbones, a pointed chin. Her skin was tan, leathery, with deep smile creases at the corners of her eyes.

"I'm Cat," she said. "I saw you talking to Sid, who probably told you to get the word from Abe. But as you can see, old Abe isn't up to anything. There's nothing he can tell you that I can't tell better, since I'm probably old enough to be your mother."

"Not that old!" He thought of the phone call.

She laughed. "I like you," she said.

Paul felt suddenly brave. "You're right," he said, "I'm starved. I've got a mess kit. Where'll I start? What's best?"

"Where you begin depends on how fast you want to get going."

Paul didn't know what she meant so he didn't say anything. He unhooked his mess kit from his belt and started toward the fire.

She went on. "The beans are herbed, that's why they smell like a spring flower market. No chili, no red pepper, just herbs by the fistful. Sid and I did the beans. The stew is laced and it kind of comes at you slow." She patted his arm, grinned and started toward Sid, leaving Paul alone with the strange crowd, the strange food. But a few feet away she turned and said, "Watch out for the dip."

You haven't kissed me yet, Paul. I thought you would while we were at the point. I guess you're scared. I know I am. But not the way I was before. I keep being afraid you won't still like me. I suppose that's silly. Nobody expects a person to be so pure anymore.

It wasn't just Roy. I don't know why I liked Reggie. I can't stand to look at him now. I met him after I got moved to the slow Spanish class. I think I felt sorry for him because the teacher picked on him. I asked him how come. He said, "All the teachers hate me. They don't like people who are different." I invited him to walk home with Danny and Barb and me. He had a nice smile, and he held my

95

hand. Nobody'd held my hand since you'd left. It felt good. I thought Barb would like having Danny to herself for a bit.

I found out that day Reggie took a lot of pills. He offered some to Barb and Danny and me. I pulled my hand away fast then. I'd been in the clinic a few weeks before when a boy was brought in on a stretcher from an overdose of something.

Barb said to him, "I'm not dumb enough to take something you scraped out of some gutter, Reggie. Where'd you get them?" He didn't answer her.

"What do they do?" I asked him.

He looked at his empty hand. "Not much," he said. "They just make you feel good." Barb and I talked about it later.

"The thing is," she told me, "you've got to protect yourself." She was always so reasonable, so knowledgeable. "Just like drinking or smoking. Do it somewhere where it won't matter if you get wobbly."

"Where's that?" I asked her.

"Home," Barb said.

"You're kidding," I said. "You mean your parents know everything you do?"

"Sure," Barb told me. "They know kids want to experiment. They told me they tried everything when they were my age. They just don't want me getting hurt. The only reason we have to go in the shed is so Mimi doesn't see us. Mom and Dad don't want her starting stuff just because she sees me doing it."

I can't tell you how that made me feel. It was like being emptied out. Home was where I could do nothing, where every minute I had to pretend, where lying became a way of life.

I knew they even searched my room sometimes. Sometimes a book would disappear.

I was so mad the day a copy of Lady Chatterley's Lover

disappeared. I'd borrowed it and forgotten to hide it, and now I'd have to buy a new one, or ask them to give it back. I'd only half-finished. At dinner Daddy told a funny story about somebody who didn't know what a tire was, because of course Daddy still calls it "tar." I laughed but then said I didn't like having my books disappear.

He got puffy and red, and Mom got that long look. They talked at me about good and bad books for kids. I like all kinds, sad ones, long ones, and sexy ones, and they don't have to be written for kids, either. I can get lost in a good book. So it wasn't fair for him to be telling me good and bad. I listened for a while and let what they said roll off. But when he started in on how books suggested things, I exploded.

"Nobody ever got raped by a book," I said.

That did it for that night. I got excused. He didn't like my language. Imagine him saying that.

That Sunday in church I was listening to the gulls, wondering where you were, worrying because of what had happened that week. All during the sermon I was thinking of you. The minister talked about the lesson to be learned from all those people poisoning themselves in Jonestown. That was so horrible. I can't imagine poisoning myself for anyone. He said how it was important to perceive the true God and not be misled by false prophets. I kept hearing those gulls and thinking about what you might say. Everyone thought they knew the truth for someone else. Daddy thought you were so bad, and I knew you weren't. What if you'd gone off with some group like that? It didn't sound like you. I wasn't really afraid you were dead. But if you weren't, I couldn't understand why you never came back.

I didn't think I knew the truth for anyone else; I don't know it for myself either. All I knew for sure was that Mom and Daddy were wrong about a lot of people. They were happy to let me walk home with Barb after church. It

97

never occurred to them that Reggie and Danny would be waiting at the corner, or that there was a roll of paper in my left shoe and some grass in my right.

That summer I tried to get Daddy to let me go away to camp with Barb. Even Mom thought it was a good idea. But I flunked Spanish, so Reggie and I ended up in summer school together. I had to make up the Spanish and he had to make up everything. Reggie wasn't smart, and he wasn't good-looking; he wasn't you, Paul. Nobody was. But I didn't know where you were.

TEN

When Paul woke, he didn't know where he was. He'd lost something. He studied the platform over his head. A rusty pipe ran its length. What had he lost?

His way.

You know the way, Paul.

No. Not that. Details began to filter back. He had found Paradise. *Peace!* He remembered Sid's greeting and some woman saying, "I like you."

Amy! He'd lost Amy. He rolled onto his side and searched among the inert forms near him. None looked familiar.

Awake now, he crawled out of his sleeping bag and out from under the bus. The bus. Another detail.

He stretched, feeling the hot sun on his neck. Already above the treetops, it promised to superheat the air by mid-afternoon. The bean pot was empty. The fires were out. People lay here and there—dawn after a cinema battle. Even the bird calls sounded staged. No faces were familiar. When he saw the empty bucket lying on its side, he remembered dipping an end of bread into the sauce. And because it tasted so good, because he felt so free, so light-headed, and saw such a befuddlement of color, he dipped it again and again.

Now he remembered the stream. He headed for the

trees. In a clearing with a good rock ledge, he rolled up his jeans and stood in the cool water. Cupping his hands, he splashed his face. He heard a man's voice over the sound of the stream, then a woman's.

"Pleasure is oft a visitant . . ."

Amy. He followed the voices downstream, around a bend. There she was with two other people.

"Hi," he said. "I thought I'd lost you."

"Hi yourself. You know you can't."

"But I missed you last night. Where were you?"

"Oh, up and away. Listen: A *lovely tale of human life we'll read./ And . . ."*

"Does she always run on like that?" the man asked.

"Jerry's telling me the story of his life," Amy explained.

Jerry was a sharp-faced man, half-old, half-evil-looking, with a few days' growth on his chin and grayish stringy hair. Over his frayed pin-striped shirt he wore a fringed suede vest covered with slogan buttons, old ones that told of history going years back. "BAN THE BOMB." "FLOWER POWER." "IMPEACH NIXON." Joe had left a whole box of buttons in his desk, Paul remembered.

"Who's that?" Paul asked. Lying across Jerry's lap, her face in perfect repose as if she was modeling for some mattress ad, was the most beautiful girl Paul had ever seen. Jerry stroked the place where her hair met her cheek.

"That's Ellie," Amy said.

Ellie's face was a perfect oval. She had wide lips, pale thick eyebrows. Her wheat-blond hair, parted down the middle, was in two long thick braids. Fine hairs that wouldn't be caught fringed her forehead. Her faded paisley dress covered all but her bare feet, which were curled together as if to keep each other company. She looked as young as Mary Lou.

"Park," Jerry said, pointing to the mossy ground. Without being able to pull his eyes from the sleeping girl, Paul

100

sat down. Jerry continued his story. His high-pitched voice scratched like a needle on one of Jojo's old 78's in the Cape house.

"The day I found him beating on my two kid brothers with his leather belt, I could have killed him. Mom and I pulled him off, but we couldn't hold him. She busted an iron skillet on his head and called the cops. They locked him up, dried him out while we had a few days' peace. I begged Mom to throw him out for good, but sober he'd be sweet and she'd let him in again. Two beers later all the mean would bust out of him. I split when I was twelve."

"What happened to your brothers?" Amy asked.

"They got out soon as they could take care of themselves. Only Mom stuck. She'll never quit him."

Paul didn't know whether to believe even half the story. It sounded awful, but phony too. He remembered Mr. Siddons. If one man beat a puppy, another might beat his children. The newspapers were full of such stories.

"One day he hurt me so bad I crawled out. A friend picked me up and took me to a house. Gave me a fix for the pain."

"Did it help?" Amy asked.

"Yeah, but it hooked me too." He shook his head.

"You do drugs now?" Paul asked.

"Not me. Never again. No stuff. No needles. Acid's something else, but there's two bad things in this world, two that get you by the short hairs. Heroin and alcohol. Remember that, kid, when you think of messing around. Nobody here uses that stuff."

"How'd you get off it?" Amy asked.

"Cat and Sid found me nodding one night. Knew where I was 'cause they'd been there too."

Paul didn't say a word. Acid. So that's where he'd been last night, that's what had wiped him out. He'd known a couple of empty-headed kids who'd bragged about tripping

101

on it. But he'd never even been curious. Only an idiot would take stuff that lost him his senses, Paul figured. Now he'd done it himself. He began to shake. Like the first day he drove alone after he got his license and a huge trailer truck ran a light and almost hit him. He'd had to pull off the road and sit for twenty minutes until he stopped shaking.

Ellie opened her eyes, rubbed them, and sat up.

"You okay, baby?" Jerry asked.

"Mmmm." Then, seeing Paul and Amy, she smiled and said, "Good morning," as if she'd known them all her life.

She stood up. Tall, broad-shouldered, and wide-hipped, she moved almost in slow motion. She reminded Paul of a girl in one of those Christmas cards with snowflakes on it, standing in her nightgown in front of a tree. How long had she been with this group? Maybe she lived nearby, he thought. Maybe she'd come for the feast. Feast. It was hardly that.

"You live near here?" he asked hopefully.

"No," Jerry answered for her. "Ellie's one of us. She's been with the Family for years."

Not true! She was too young. It was okay for him to be here, a vacation, a lark. And Amy was old enough to know what she wanted. But not Ellie. Jerry must be twice her age. Had she done hard drugs too?

As if it were the most natural thing in the world, Ellie reached down to her ankles, lifted the hem of her dress, and pulled it over her head. Naked, she walked calmly into the creek. She floated as if she and the creek belonged to each other, her arms encircling a rock, her braids trailing along her back.

I'm not here, Paul told himself. This isn't happening.

Amy stripped and followed Ellie into the creek. Paul laughed. A swim sure seemed like a good idea. He took off his shirt.

"Come on in," Amy called. "It's cooler here."

102

"More mellow," Ellie said, blowing bubbles.

Drifting downstream, Paul stayed in the water after the girls and Jerry went up. He listed his confusions. He felt nourished by more than food, warmed and welcomed, but shocked too, and incredibly aroused. He didn't know what was real, what was dream, what might be a trick the acid had played on his mind. Maybe this cool, rushing stream was a hallucination, and he'd wake up in Rocky Shores hearing, *This the boy, sir?*

Come home now, Paul.

He let the water rush over him until he stopped thinking.

When Paul finally climbed up the mossy bank, he felt good; clean and alive. But he couldn't find his clothes. He searched through the trees. Then he saw Jerry stepping into his jeans. Damn.

"Hey, watch where you put that foot." Paul carefully kept his tone light.

"Why?" Jerry looked up.

"They're my only pants. I need 'em."

"I didn't know you cared." Jerry dropped the jeans. Paul realized he'd stumbled over another intimacy of this family. Nothing bothered them, neither time nor place nor possession. He wasn't sure he needed to be that free. He certainly didn't want anyone else wearing his pants. Besides, what was left of his money was in his right front pocket. He did need that.

A blur of days later he sat on a water-padded rock ledge and viewed the ravine through the falls. His thighs took the full brunt of the torrent. Stinging backspray massaged his face and chest. Water raced between his fingers spread flat on the stone. He forced his eyes open, recording in his mind the shattered landscape. His eyes were a camera, recording the kaleidoscopic vision where pine and spruce were trees no longer, nor creek bottom distinguished from moss, ivy, and fern-strewn banks, sky known only by its blinding, flickering light. Then he was running, running to keep up with Joe. Joe pulled him so hard he flew over the sidewalk. Cheering, chanting crowds closed in, crushing the breath out of him. He held on to Joe's belt. "Are you all right, Paulie? We'll go home soon . . . don't tell Dad . . ."

He had to go home.

"Are you all right? Come on, Paul."

Someone tugged at his arm. He tried to pull loose. Hands gripped his bicep. Through the stream over his eyes he saw a woman struggling, saying something, her mouth opening and closing. Cat.

She put her lips to his ear and yelled, "I need you."

Reluctantly he stood up. Out of the torrent he felt his nakedness and nearly escaped back into the waterfall. But Cat held him tight and led him to dry land.

"I thought I'd never get you out of there." Hand in hand they climbed to the top of a boulder, where sun warmed the rock. He sat quickly, hugging his knees, hiding himself, not looking at her.

"What did you want me for?"

She settled beside him. "You'd been there for hours. I was afraid you'd drown."

"You sound like my mother."

"No!" she said sharply. He'd never heard any of the Sunshine Family speak sharply before. "Not yours, not anyone's mother. Not that trip."

"What's the matter?" he asked.

She lay back on her elbows and didn't answer.

He'd been with the Family a week, and was used to that treatment. Questions went unanswered; you said what came into your mind. Words like shooting stars missed any target. He didn't mind; he'd gotten to like it.

He began to dry out; warmed by the sun above and the hot rock below, his flesh tingled.

She stood up suddenly. "Let's go," she said.

"Where?"

"I need you to drive me to town."

They crossed the pasture to camp. The bus, that crazily painted bus, beckoned him. Like home.

"Can't Sid go?"

"No."

"Or Jerry?"

"He's out of it. Besides, it's your turn. Everyone does his share." Communal living. Paul thought suddenly of Jojo. Not quite free. He'd been glad not to be asked to drive. Now, he thought, she was accepting him as a full-fledged family member. He had to take his turn.

"Okay," he said, "but I better get my pants."

She smiled and punched his arm. "You learn fast," she said. "I like having you here."

I saw your mother at the library one day. I'd seen her a bunch of times before, but I never knew who she was. I overheard her talking to another librarian, and she said something about a phone call. I stopped and listened. She sounded so upset, and she said, "There was only the one call, and I'm afraid I handled it all wrong. He'd lied to me." She went on to say how you'd missed so much school, and she never heard from you again. I was sure it was your mother, and I was dying to tell her who I was, but I didn't dare. I was surprised about your lying. I didn't think you'd ever do that. It made me wonder about me. Two years ago I didn't think I'd ever lie to my mother either.

I stopped seeing Reggie after he made me get that job. He didn't really make me, but he was always out of money. I thought it would be fun. I piled my hair on my head, said I was sixteen, and they believed me. It was on the other side of town, so I managed to work for two weeks before Mom and Daddy found out. Reggie waited for me until the day Roy and I got off at the same time, and he saw us come out laughing.

I felt sorry for Reggie. He did get picked on, but he wasn't much fun. Feeling sorry for someone isn't the same as liking him.

After Daddy sent you away, I was so angry, and for a while I felt sorry for myself. Barb and Danny helped me out of that. I'd never feel sorry for you, even though Daddy did hurt you. I never want to, either.

Sometimes I feel sorry for Mom, though, when Daddy is impossible, or when she tries to do something I want and has to choose between us. But then I think she could stand up for what she believes. If she'd been stronger, maybe I could have gone to camp with Barb. I wouldn't even have met Roy, then. But you can't live your life with ifs.

ELEVEN

"Take the stream at a pretty good clip," Cat said. "Then we won't get stuck halfway." Paul followed her advice and gunned the motor. Water splashed through the floorboards of the old Ford pickup, but they didn't get stuck. On the whole, Paul found Cat's advice worth listening to. She offered it to everyone. Some followed it, some didn't. Although she naturally took on the role of mother in the Family, he was careful not to mention it again.

"This baby needs a ring job," he said, noticing the trail of black smoke.

"Sid knows. He'd do it if he could get help, and some parts."

"I'd help," Paul said, "but I guess I won't be here."

"I guess you won't," Cat said.

They drove in silence back over the dirt road Paul and Amy had walked more than a week before. But when they came to the macadam, Cat began to talk. She talked all the way to town.

She told Paul she'd picked up with Sid and Jerry in Berkeley ten years before, after she'd been fired from her first teaching job. "I was supposed to lead a discussion of *The Merchant of Venice* the day Martin Luther King was shot."

"April fourth," Paul said. "My birthday. I was six and my mother cried. I'd never seen her cry."

"It was bad then," Cat went on. "I went down to Union Square but a bunch of Hell's Angels were there, threatening people, so I took the bus to Berkeley and ran into a demonstration. It was bad everywhere. The power-seekers were yelling at the peace-lovers. How could anything good ever happen when the best leaders got shot? In my life, two Kennedys and now King. I was the first person in my family to get through college, but I couldn't even keep a job. The principal had walked into my class while a boy was standing on a desk trying to get the class to strike. I couldn't control them. I didn't know what to do.

"Sid and Jerry were leaning against a parked van, passing a joint back and forth. I'd known Sid from one of my classes, so I joined them. They told me about a group they knew that stayed out of cities where so much trouble was and lived by the only truth, peace, brotherhood, and Mother Nature. We decided to split.

"Jerry said you helped him get off hard drugs. Was that before or after?"

Cat looked at him sharply. "Jerry helped me too," she said. Paul was startled.

"And the acid, isn't that dangerous? Or did Mother Nature devise that too?"

"We don't lay it on anyone. That's the whole point. You're free to do whatever you want."

Paul drove in silence. He was free, more than he'd ever been. No one expected anything of him. Then why was he worried? What Cat had done or not done way back was no concern of his.

As if reading his mind, she put her hand over his. "Relax. Don't worry about it. People do what they do. Drift or anchor. Dream or write. Just do what's natural and don't hurt anyone."

"Have you ever thought of leaving the Family?" Paul asked. "Could you quit and go home?"

"Where's that? Not the city, thank you, no. I wouldn't plug back into that power-tripping world for millions. Everything's programmed, even God. Art, music, sex, religion—the bottom line has replaced all other truths."

"Sid said a lot more people used to show up. He told me 1976 was a big year."

"That's not important, how big we are. Holding to our ideals is the thing. Sid and I—we love nature. We're retribalizing. The Indians lived here a long time and didn't hurt the land or wipe out herds or turn virgin forests into sun decks. We need very little: transportation so we can follow the sun; water; a handful of rice or beans; space."

"What about the bus?"

"It's sort of a symbol. We use it for a kitchen. Unfortunately, that one has no motor, so I'm tracking other wheels."

Paul slowed behind a truck overloaded with hay.

"There are so many lost people in this beautiful country, lonely kids like you or Ellie or Amy. We meet them everywhere and want to be ready."

"I'm not lost. I'm on vacation."

"That's not what you said the other night." He passed the hay truck. "It sounded as if you'd left a mess of baggage behind when you struck out. Don't worry. We won't turn our backs on you."

Paul gripped the wheel hard. He didn't like thinking about that baggage. The pickup swerved.

"What's up?" Cat asked.

"I just remembered. There's somebody I really turned my back on."

"Listen!" Cat's voice became hard. "One thing you'd better learn. We've no time for guilt. There are no courts or judges in our green field. Pull into that gas station." He did and stopped by the tank. "Sit tight," she said, took something from the back, and went into the station.

While he waited, Paul mentally composed a letter he'd write to Mary Lou as soon as he got back. *I've found a family,* he'd say, *that I'd really like you to meet. Very beautiful people, that show each other lots of love, really from the heart. They don't expect a person to do what he can't or doesn't feel is right to do. They don't believe in guilt, or polluting Mother Earth. They follow the sun. Here they live in a green field by a beautiful clear creek. By the time I get back home, they'll be in Arkansas. . . . I'll call you somehow.*

Cat came out, filled up the tank, and climbed in. "Let's go," she said.

"Hey, don't you have to pay for gas in this town?"

"I paid," Cat said. "Barter. We grew a fine crop this summer." Paul started. Smoking pot was one thing, but selling was another. Was barter the same as selling? He pushed the thought away. He hadn't done either one.

The town was two blocks long. Like dozens he'd been through on the way west, the main road widened out a little; there was a café, a general store, a liquor store, and a feed store. No sidewalk, just a few frame houses that let onto the street.

At the general store Cat got some salt, rice, oats, barley, dry beans, lentils, and peas. She asked about the hardware Sid needed. The man said to try the feed store. Then she asked if he had any old books.

"There's a coupla bundles out back I'm about to tear the covers off and dump," he said.

"How about leaving the covers on and dumping them on me?"

"But I get credit."

"I'll pay what you get for credit. What would it be?"

"Maybe a dime or so on each one."

"I'll pay," Cat said.

Her eyes lit up when she saw the books. He counted

110

them slowly. "There's twenty-eight. Probably worth maybe three bucks. I'll only charge you two."

She dug into her dress pocket and pulled out a little brown purse. Paul guessed that if she spent two dollars she wouldn't have enough for the groceries. The storekeeper didn't look like the type to accept even good grass in barter. Sid needed parts for the pickup, and Ellie'd asked for thread.

The hungry look on Cat's face reminded Paul of the boys in Charley's class waiting for a chance to sail. He took two dollars out of his pocket. "I'll be eating off you the rest of the week. Let me buy the books."

"Great! I'll pay you back."

Paul paid for the groceries too. On the way home, Cat said, they'd stop at Knecht's farm. "They give us the remains from their stand sales. Whatever they can't eat themselves, we take. The sour milk and the wilted lettuce. We use everything. People are so wasteful."

Paul was impressed. He could learn a lot from her, he thought. About food and gardening. He thought the way she felt about the money-mad aspect of the world was interesting. But he couldn't imagine living like this, sleeping out all the time and scrounging food from farmers' surplus for ten years. He looked at her tanned face, the lines around her mouth. She must be over thirty.

They got the car parts from the feed store. Cat told Paul to drive to a white frame house at the end of the street. "There's a kid I've been tutoring, teaching to read. He's eleven, retarded. And I think they've got a van they'd be willing to part with. Wait here."

She knocked on the door and talked to the man who opened it, then followed him inside. A gray van was parked by the garage. Could she trade a van for a few reading lessons? She was more talented than he'd imagined. Well, it was none of his business, he thought. Or, as Johanna would say, "Hidy ho, let the wind blow. So long as your feet can move, you've somewhere to go."

That Johanna, every time he saw her, she was dancing. Hidy ho. This was some vacation. If he'd planned it ahead, he couldn't have found a crazier bunch of people to spend two weeks with. Some change over Rocky Shores. *We have no time for guilt.* A good change. He felt weightless.

Suddenly Cat was at the window, her hand on his arm. "Drive on home, Paul. I've got a bargain. Tell Sid to pull it together. I'll be home by sundown."

She was excited. He opened his mouth to ask if he should stop at the farm, but she put her finger on his lips. Like a kiss. "Scoot," she said. "Take care of my books. And thanks."

At camp he found Sid with his head under the yawning hood of the bus. Paul looked inside the empty compartment. "If you could get hold of a motor, do you think you could get the thing to run?"

Sid shook his head. "I don't know. Doubt it. The front axle's broken. I don't know about the camshaft."

"That's easy to check."

Sid nodded. "We need something big to get to Arkansas. It won't be warm here much longer."

"Cat's got a van. She told me to tell you."

"Good Cat."

"When do you think you'll leave?"

"Soon. It depends on the moon."

"The moon?"

"Waning gibbous is best." Sid was talking riddles again. "Why?" Paul asked.

Sid looked at him as if he were stupid. "There's an old Indian legend . . ." His words trailed off. Paul realized his eyes were unfocused. "Where's Cat?" he asked.

"I told you. Getting a van. I left her at a house. She said to tell you to pull it together."

112

Suddenly snapping into focus, Sid clapped his hands. "Okay. We'll have a meeting. Round everyone up." He turned to help Paul unload the pickup and found Cat's books. He laughed. "She'd rather read than eat."

While they put the supplies in the bus, Paul wondered why it was best to travel under a waning gibbous, what the legend was that Sid seemed to have forgotten. He'd ask Cat when she got back, but he wasn't sure he'd get an answer.

Cat wasn't back by sundown, nor in time for supper. Amy and Jerry strolled in from the creek hand in hand. Paul looked away. He didn't like Jerry. Ellie sat Indian fashion sewing a gingham patch on her paisley dress. Sid lit the fire and cut some vegetables into the pot. Abe hauled water from the creek. You never knew how Sid's stew pot of fresh vegetables would taste, but when you were hungry, and Paul always was, it didn't matter much what you ate. There were always beans soaking for the next day. Where was Cat? No one seemed to worry except Paul.

For the first time since he'd been with them, Paul was lonely. Seeing Amy and Jerry started it. He wasn't attracted to Amy. He'd traveled with her alone for two and a half days, even shared his sleeping bag with her, waking to find her curled like a baby against him, without trying anything. But he'd been stunned when he saw her naked. He didn't like the idea of Jerry's hands on her.

He hadn't always had sex on his mind so much. Now all he could think about were naked bodies. He wondered if he stayed here much longer whether he'd get used to nakedness.

Suddenly he realized that everyone was sitting in a circle near the fire except him. Even Johanna had stopped dancing. Sid perched on an apple crate, which put him a little above everyone.

"This is the force," he said in a low voice. Sid was a born leader, Paul decided, even when he didn't make sense.

"Hidy ho," Johanna said. "Glue us in, Sid. I need to center a bit."

"I think it's time to roll. How do you all feel about that?"

"I feel fine," Johanna said. "Let's blow with the wind." She put her hands on her cheeks and let out little whistling sounds.

Jerry said, "It's not that I won't go with the flow, but there are a few tributaries along the creek I haven't explored. Perhaps in a few weeks?"

"Abe?" Sid asked.

Abe plucked a stem of grass and stuck it between his teeth. He was a heavy-shouldered hulk of a boyish man, maybe nineteen, maybe twenty-nine. He never got hot, cold, or bothered. He wore the same gaping bib overalls day after day. His broad blunt-fingered hands were strong, and he volunteered to do anything heavy. Abe and Johanna were a pair. When Johanna danced, Abe rocked in front of her. When she stopped, he stopped. When she sat, he sat. He agreed with anyone.

"I could roll right now, or I could stay a month. It all depends." His voice was surprisingly high for such a big guy.

Sid nodded. "Ellie?"

Ellie looked up from her sewing and smiled. "Yes?"

"How do you feel about heading south?"

"That's fine. I'm ready. Only, please let me have my sewing. I need to do something with my hands."

"Of course, sewing is fine," Sid said gently.

She stretched like a cat being petted.

To the group Sid said, "There's one thing more. We're short on the long green. Who'll go to work?"

"Didn't we collect any during the feast?" Jerry asked.

"Some, but not enough. Could you work for a few days, Jerry? Abe? The Knecht farm might need help with the haying."

Jerry shook his head. "I don't think we ought to move

114

yet. I don't like the idea. Old man Knecht doesn't treat his hands right. He's got a mean gleam in his eye."

"You have to get past the negativity, Jerry," Johanna said.

"I'll get the food stamps. You want to come, Johanna?"

"All right. You can all go for stamps. We'll get work on the road. Haying's just started here, it'll be in full swing down south," Sid said.

Ellie smiled. "Tell me what to do, Sid. I don't mind work."

"It's all decided, then. That's good."

Paul couldn't remember anyone deciding anything.

"I didn't ask you or Amy, Paul, because I didn't think you planned to stay with us."

"Right," Paul said automatically. "I promised Amy I'd get her to Colorado. Then I'll head east. My school starts in a week."

"School?" Ellie said as if remembering something in the distant past. "I didn't know you went to school, Paul. That's wonderful."

He was embarrassed. "I was. I mean, I am. It'll take me most of a week to get there."

"Do just as you like," Sid said. "Though you're welcome to travel with us. Before you go, maybe you'd help me tune the pickup. Abe, you could fill and seed the slit trenches, and, Jerry, you walk to town with the girls for the stamps."

"Walk! Hell, Sid, we can't walk all that far. Why can't you drive us?"

"I suppose I could, and let you walk home." Sid stirred the stew.

Johanna started her dance. Abe said, "Man, I'm hollow," and took a bowl from his back pocket. Sid filled that and another for Ellie. Amy and Jerry filled one bowl and fed each other. Paul dug out his mess kit and helped himself. Pairs had changed. Where was Cat?

After I had to quit the job, I got back in Mom's good graces by taking Jamie to the beach in the afternoons. It was something to do. He'd play with his pals and I'd find somebody to talk to. Roy often came by after work and bought us cones. Jamie never told. He thought Roy was fun and funny. Jamie's always been neat.

I wouldn't smoke dope with Roy. He wanted me to, but I was afraid of being swept away. Some things bothered me about him. We'd watch the sailboats and the kids, but he'd never talk about anything we saw, only about him and me. He never noticed anything.

I read some books that summer about people who were sick in their minds. They fascinated me. I tried to tell Roy about one: I Never Promised You a Rose Garden. I explained how discovering why that girl hurt herself was more exciting than any spacy movie, Star Wars or whatever.

All he said was how crazy he was, if I liked crazies. Crazy for me. "You want the world upside down?" he said, and stood on his head right there on the beach. "Okay, I'll turn the whole world over for you." I couldn't help laughing. I let him kiss me. But I wouldn't smoke with him. After he left, I'd tell Mom I was going to the library. I'd slip into Barb's shed, even though she was away, and smoke by myself. To calm me down.

When Barb got home from camp, I told her about Roy.

"He sounds sexy," Barb said. "Be careful. Don't let him laugh you into doing what you don't want to do."

"I don't know what I want to do. When he kisses me, I want to do everything, but . . ."

That's when Barb told me she and Danny had started sleeping together. I was stunned. I stared at Barb to see if she looked different.

116

"When you truly love someone, you'll know it. You don't think about right and wrong," Barb said.

"Aren't you afraid you'll get pregnant?"

"We're careful."

"What do you do?"

"After the first couple of times, I told Mom. She took me to the doctor. I take the pill. She doesn't think I ought to be on it long, but for now it's less clumsy than a diaphragm and she thinks it's safer."

"You told your mom! And I suppose she said fine, just fine."

"She didn't say it was or wasn't fine. I'd already done it. I didn't ask her permission, for heaven's sake. I mean, what we do is between Danny and me."

"What did your mother say?"

"She said I ought to be protected."

I can't tell you how lonely that made me feel, Paul. Barb had Danny and could tell her mother everything. She said, "There's nothing I can't tell Mom about. She wants me to go to her if I get in trouble."

Where would I go if I got in trouble? I thought and thought about letting Roy do what he wanted—what I want too when his hands are all over me. Maybe I'd even go away with him.

But tell Mother and Daddy? I mean, any little thing I tell them, or they find out, will start the mess all over again.

TWELVE

Paul couldn't sleep. Ellie and Sid had long since disappeared. Amy and Jerry had gone to the creek. Paul had gotten tired of watching Johanna dance, knowing she'd dance till she dropped by the fire and lie by the dead coals alone or in Abe's arms until morning. So Paul had retreated under the bus. He lay in his sleeping bag homesick, confused, a sadness deepening in him he didn't understand.

They'd passed a joint around but he hadn't inhaled. He'd asked Amy if she wanted to go on to Colorado, but she was vague. Jerry stuck to her as if rubber bands held them together. Disgusted, Paul watched them kiss, a long soul kiss, but he couldn't look away. Hell, it was none of his business what Amy did.

What did he want? Colorado didn't beckon him now. The continental divide was another dead dream. He'd go straight home, he decided. He remembered the letter he was going to write Mary Lou. No sense in that now. He'd find her at school and scheme some way to see her.

He'd told Sid he'd travel with them as far as Cedar Rapids, where the Family would turn south. He'd be home easily in time for registration.

The good classes filled up early. Shop filled in the spring. If he was late, he'd lose his place. Teachers were hard on kids coming in late. Any tests they'd missed came off their grade. New people had a tough time too—Mary Lou had. He'd said he'd go home, and he'd go.

Forcing his eyes closed, he wished for sleep, but his mind wheeled off at its own pace, refusing to wind down. He'd enjoy a few more days with the Family. He'd help Sid with the pickup; he'd enjoy a few more hours looking at Ellie.

He'd come upon her under the apple tree one day, brushing out her hair. He sat on a low branch and watched her. She brushed and brushed until it was all shining silk. Then, like a harpist's, her fingers did wonderful things together, going so fast he couldn't follow them. The hair flipped this way and that and came out above her fingers in a thick, perfect braid. When she was finished, he said, "That's a miracle. I wish I could see you do it again."

"You can," she said, took off the two rubber bands, and brushed her hair out straight again. Then she did the miracle with her fingers once more. He felt as if she'd given him a private concert.

"No one's ever done anything like that for me just because I asked. Thanks, Ellie."

"What a pity," she said.

He opened his eyes, surprised at how brightly the cold white light of a rising moon lit the camp. He crawled from under the bus and saw, just over the field, a fine fat moon. Waning gibbous, Sid had said, was best for travel. The moon was ready. Was he?

It was too beautiful to hide from. He pulled out his sleeping bag and wondered where he wanted to put it. Not by the dying fire. Not near Sid's tepee. He was lonely, but he wanted some distance from these strange people who, in only a week, had become so important he couldn't get them out of his head. He walked up toward the apple tree. At a particularly soft stretch of grass he dropped his bag and leaned against the fence.

He was about to try to sleep again when he heard a motor and the crunch of wheels on dry leaves.

Cat climbed out of the van. She walked straight up the gentle slope, slipped her hand into the crook of his elbow. They didn't speak. Finally she put a joint to her lips. He lit it. She inhaled deeply and handed it to him. He pulled smoke into his lungs. Why hadn't he wanted this earlier? Why did he take it now? He didn't know. He let himself exhale slowly. She hugged his arm. He could feel her breast. He didn't move.

"You're not high," she said.

"No."

"You're not sleepy. What were you waiting for?"

"I don't know. Sid had a meeting."

"I know."

He wondered if she were jealous of Sid and Ellie. He knew he mustn't ask.

He said, "Sid decided to roll. I'm going with you as far as Cedar Rapids. Then I'll go home to my family."

She was silent. She drew on the joint. Finally she said, "This is home. This is the Family."

He felt her hurt. She thought he held himself apart, as if he were looking at them, not a spy but a peeper. She wanted him to want her. He didn't. But it hadn't made sense either when he said "to my family." What was his family now?

His mother: Was he ready to hear her cry?

Jojo: Part of another life, another time.

Joe: Somewhere in California, a distant relative.

Dad: Nowhere.

What drew him back to Rocky Shores?

Mary Lou. But he couldn't even talk to her on the phone.

He took another long drag and some of the sadness floated away. The fat moon swelled. Cat's eyes reflected its light. He thought: This moon is getting bigger and bigger.

120

He felt Cat's hands on his chest, under his shirt. He tried to kiss her.

"No," she said. "Not yet. Not that yet. I'll show you." She took his hands and led him. She touched him, then guided his hands to touch her. Later she slept with her head on his chest. Cat.

The morning went according to plan, except that Cat drove the new van to town with Jerry, Johanna, Ellie, and Amy. Sid and Paul worked on the pickup. If the van drove well, they'd tow the pickup. If not, they'd tow the van. But now they had wheels enough to get them to Arkansas, and space for the strays they might pick up along the way. They'd leave in two days, Sid said, and plan for the next big meeting en route. Johanna and Cat were to write the notice.

By noon Sid had the top of the motor block off so they could reset the valves. Paul had the carburetor apart, the clean pieces in his mess kit. Abe had filled most of the trenches. They broke for a swim, a lunch of bread and tomatoes, a cool drink of creek water. As they walked back to camp, two men with rifles came across the field.

Smiling his broadest, Sid raised his hand palm outward and said, "Peace."

"Peace shit," the smaller man said. They looked grim and didn't lower their rifles. Paul's heart pounded. Abe hooked his hands in his overalls and rocked.

Hardly moving his lips, the short man said, "Get your pals outen our jail and the lotoyou outen this town, hear?"

Sid lowered his hand. "Who's in jail?"

"The whole filthy bunch. Damn lucky they ain't dead, ask me. Loaded with mar-i-jua-na cigarettes too." He pronounced each syllable carefully. "Corruptin' our children. Bustin' up homes. Now, git."

Still calm, Sid said, "You better tell me the whole story."

"Ain't no story. Anyone can see you're bad stuff."

"We haven't harmed anyone or the land," Sid said. "As a matter of fact, we are planning to leave day after tomorrow. We're seeding the—"

"Just blow! No talk. There's a price of ten dollars on each of 'em. Call it bail or a fine or whatever. Forty bucks'll spring 'em. So long as you clear out tonight, and *stay out,* we won't file charges."

Sid said, "Our pickup's in pieces. How'll we get to town?"

The men turned to each other. "All right. Ride with us."

Paul stayed close to Sid. Abe hung back. Did Sid have forty dollars? If he didn't . . . Suddenly the full force of what had happened hit Paul. It wasn't just Jerry in the town jail, but the girls. Paul had never been inside a jail. He imagined a dark and filthy place from the movies he'd seen.

When they walked into the drab concrete-block building with its scuffed tan walls, they heard someone singing. "Hidy ho, let the wind blow!" They found Ellie and Cat and Johanna with a bucket of gray water, singing while they mopped the cells, the hall, and the little bathroom. Jerry sat on the floor of one of the cells glowering.

"What the hell?" the sheriff said.

"We didn't have anything else to do," Ellie said. "But we didn't know where to dump the trash." She pointed to a pile at the end of the hall.

"I'll get it," the tall man said.

Cat told Sid that they'd turned Jerry down for stamps and he got so mad he broke into the back of the liquor store before she knew where he'd gone. "He only took a pint, but I'm afraid he's finished it. We were still signing papers when we heard the ruckus. By then it was too late."

"How much did they get on you?" Sid asked.

"Not much."

"Pay up and get that sonofabitch out of this state," the sheriff said, shoving a paper across the counter.

Sid searched first one of his pockets, then another, coming up with a single here, a five there. He counted out the crumpled bills. At fourteen he said, "Listen, we'll clean the whole town, pick up trash, sweep the gutters. In lieu of the long green, what about—?"

"No way," the sheriff said. "Cash or they stay."

Sid pulled hard at his beard. "It's hard to leave town if half of us is in jail."

The sheriff's lips were a thin, straight line. "We'll get rid of them if you can't. No problem. Send 'em over to the county facility. If they get booked, it'll take a team of fancy lawyers, a pile of money, and more'n a couple of years before they see blue sky."

Paul fingered his wad of bills. Slowly he counted out four tens and put them on the counter. Sid gave him a long look and without a word stuffed the crumpled bills back in his pocket. No one spoke. Papers were passed back and forth. Finally the sheriff nodded to the deputy, and a minute later the girls and a scowling Jerry were out in the midday sun. The sheriff stood in the doorway.

"I'll take a run out in the morning," he said. "Make sure you haven't left anyone behind."

"Where'd you park the van?" Sid asked Cat.

They loaded up at Knecht's farm with old fruit and vegetables, and skim, sweet, and sour milk. "I'll make cottage cheese out of the sour," Cat told Paul. Word of the trouble hadn't reached the farm, but one of the young boys said he'd seen the sheriff's car whiz past his field of corn and beans so fast "they musta looked like succotash." He waited for someone to laugh. Finally Paul did.

They worked all night under a waning moon. One more night, Paul thought, and you couldn't call it gibbous. They were glad for the light. Sid directed; Cat packed the van,

Ellie the pickup bed. Abe shook down the apple tree and roped the van to the pickup. Johanna stripped the bus. Paul packed the pickup parts in a bucket, wishing they'd finished the job. When they were ready, Johanna wore the steering wheel of the bus like a necklace. She liked it, she said, because it was so nice and round.

As Paul rolled his gear into his sleeping bag, he thought of the last time he'd packed up. He thought of last night with Cat. He wished he were spreading it out again. He thought of his mother, whom he hadn't called in a while. He'd see her soon enough, he thought.

"Why don't you catch some sleep in the van," Sid said, "before you're on your thumb? You've a way to go, you know."

Paul nodded. He knew. A long way home. He had fifteen dollars left. If he was lucky, that would get him to Rocky Shores. If not, well, he'd sell something.

Sid, Ellie, and Amy rode in the front of the van. Abe and Johanna chose the cab of the pickup. They left Jerry asleep in the bed. Cat and Paul stretched out in the alley she'd left clear in the back of the van. They didn't touch.

Paul thought about it. Last night Cat had taught his hands new lessons. He looked at them, held them in the air over his head. Had they learned enough? Were they a man's hands now? He put them on his stomach safely. Docile hands. Now even when the bumps and rolls on the curves might have thrown them against each other, Cat held herself to herself, apart from him, her arms crossed over her chest.

Paul fell asleep hearing in the rhythm of the wheels thumping over rough seams and patches in the old road: *You know the way.*

Heavy seas pounded the hull; wind whistled and screamed; the stays twanged; the old mast creaked. His

124

head knocked about in the cockpit, banging on the floorboards. The boat rolled. The tiller swung above his head. He grabbed but lost it. *Look out!* The sheet cracked like a dozen whips, and sails slapped about his head. A man's voice broadcast over static; a small-craft warning? No! A maniac loose on the streets, a pervert! Call the law. The sheriff had a long gun, and the muzzle pointed at Paul. Pervert! Rapist! The muzzle touched his temple; hands were all over him, pulling at his trunks, searching everywhere. *Are we lost?* The static voice yelled. *Is she lost?* Where is Mary Lou? Her naked arms reached out of the water. He didn't want to see her, but he couldn't turn his head. She cried, *Nobody cares where you go or what time you get home.* He couldn't sit up. He had to wake up, but his eyes were glued. It was only a nightmare. The boat was unmanned, adrift. Bars held him down to the cockpit floor. Mary Lou!

Suddenly the storm stopped. The dead-calm sea was silent. Paul's eyes flew open. Jojo stood frowning down at him, talking in the static weatherman's voice. Not Jojo.

Paul sat up. Sid was in the open side door of the van. It was light. The hot still air was like a wall. Paul could see an old Mobil gas tank past Sid's shoulders. Cat lay on her back, arms under her head, eyes open.

"So long, Paul," Sid said.

Cedar Rapids. Nowhere, USA. He was a long way from home. He was on his way. *Pleasure never is at home.* He would never see Amy again. Or Ellie braid her hair. *Nobody cares.*

"We'll be in New Mexico by May," Sid said. "You can find us there. We'll send you a notice."

"Can I?" He looked at Cat. Motionless, she stared straight up. He saw Ellie come out of the ladies' room.

Paul handed his last fifteen dollars to Sid. "I'll buy the gas," he said.

125

Sid studied the money, pulled at his beard, then said, "Sure, now?"

"Wake me when you're tired of driving," Paul said. Sid closed the door. In a few minutes they began to roll.

Paul didn't close his eyes or speak. He didn't touch Cat. It was dark in the van except for the spot of light that came from the one tiny window Cat hadn't packed anything against. The hum of the wheels filled his ears. He studied the ceiling, the glyphs in torn cloth, smudges, dents.

He said, "I'll call my mom at the next gas station."

"Sh-sh-sh," Cat said. He felt her finger on his lips. Like a kiss.

For six months Daddy's talked about going back to Texas. Ever since Mom found my stash—I hid it in the toilet-paper roller—he says everything bad happened because we moved. But I met you here. I don't consider that bad.

I've gotten to like the city. It's not scary once you learn your way around. I went to a Carnegie Hall concert with Barb and Danny and Reggie—yes, I still see him once in a while. I love the crowds and the wildly dressed women on Madison Avenue. We went to an art exhibit where everything was touchable. Stuff hung from the ceiling and floated over your face. We thought about putting on an exhibit in Long Island Sound where the thing was to "feel" the water, meaning everyone had to strip and swim. We had some laughs. I was glad Roy wasn't there, or he'd have been at me again about stripping. Reggie may not be much, but he isn't at me all the time.

Roy's leaving for California in October, and still wants me to go along. He's saved some money. I'd have to drop out for half a year, but I can always go back. I don't know; I'm ready to fly. I don't want to go back to Texas. I wouldn't mind living in Houston, but Daddy says no way.

California tempts me. If I act just right, maybe Daddy would let me go to college in California. I get on with him and Mom all right now. I do what they say and only smoke weekends, so my grades aren't so bad. As long as I keep what I think to myself, we don't fight.

Sometimes I think there are a whole bunch of me's, and I don't know which one is real. There's the me that's excited about anything new, the way I was that summer with you, full to bursting. I feel that way today watching you handle this boat. When I saw the movie Fame, I wanted to be a singer or dancer, some kind of artist. I loved the way those kids worked so hard for their art. But I don't have any talent. I'm not very good at anything.

That brings me to the next me, the tired one. You never met that me. When I was afraid I couldn't do something, the world seemed heavy. Trying to figure out an equation makes my head heavy. Hearing a teacher say, "You aren't trying, Mary Lou," makes me feel heavy. I've learned, though. If I say, "I'm sorry. I'll try harder," they smile as if I've done something wonderful.

If you ask me, and I hope you do, I'm not sorry for anything I've done. I've never tried to hurt anyone. I've never tried to hurt myself.

THIRTEEN

They stayed in Arkansas until the nights grew cold, then rolled on to Oklahoma. There, beside a flat red river, they had another three-day festival. Paul played host and dished up the beans, while Sid and Cat held tribal meetings. About fifty people of all ages, some with kids and some alone, ate and sang and joined their contemplative sessions about the fires. Paul didn't push the dip, but it was there.

The end of the third day a sheriff and six deputies rounded them up before they even had a chance to clean the field. They worked in a gravel pit till their hands blistered for the fines they couldn't raise. The day they left, Sid said, "When this country was established, it was envisioned as the light and the hope of the world, a place where people could gather and live in freedom. Next time we'll find a site within a national park and meet with our government's blessing and consent."

Paul washed his sore hands in the red river and wondered where or when that would be.

They towed the pickup through East Texas, and in each silent crossroads town, a square cleared in the dense forest, he wondered if Mary Lou had grown up somewhere near.

They camped west of Galveston on the hard brown sand beach where summer houses stood on stilts on a scrubby strip between the dark gulf waters and a still lagoon. Though by a sea, it didn't look like Rocky Shores. No trees, no rocks, no rise and fall. Great white herons fished in the cattails behind their camp. Motorcycles, trucks, and cars raced past them as they swam in the opaque surf or lay on the fine oil-stained sand.

The sun wheeled around and the moon grew fat and waned. Paul didn't count days or trips or the troops of people who strolled by, some stopping awhile, some shying away. He didn't count anything, or on anything. His skin turned as dark as the sand.

They piled in the van one day and drove up to Houston to visit Ellie's father. She hadn't been home in two years. They jumped in his heated pool and washed off the sand. They took hot showers. They explored his house and garden. Cat took a stack of books from his huge library and lay on the diving board reading. Ellie's father didn't seem to mind.

They found two avocados, a cucumber, half a melon, a head of lettuce, and a jar of mayonnaise in the fridge. Sid mixed it up and they dipped the salad with Doritos, and then with their fingers when the Doritos ran out.

"I've got knives and forks," Daddy said.

"We don't want to be a bother," Sid said.

"We've cleaned you out, Daddy," Ellie said.

"I'd have bought food if I'd known you were coming."

"We didn't want you to go to the trouble," Sid said.

"I don't mind the trouble," Daddy said. "I'm just glad to know you're alive, Ellie. Last I heard, you were in California."

He let them sleep on the living-room floor because their clothes were still in the washer and dryer. Paul and Ellie's father sat by the pool long after she'd fallen asleep.

"She looks like you," Paul said. "Were you blond before you got gray?"

129

"Her mother was."

"Was she always so placid? Nothing ever bothers Ellie. I never knew anyone smile so much."

"She was perfection until she met the wrong boy. Her mother should have watched her better."

"Maybe he wasn't wrong," Paul said. "Maybe you just didn't know him very well."

"He was wrong."

Awhile later Paul asked, "Where is her mother?"

"There was nothing to hold her here after Ellie ran away."

They cleaned Daddy out of cold cereal in the morning and finished his milk. Johanna cleaned out his medicine chest too. It was the biggest find in uppers and downers they'd had in ages.

While Paul and Ellie were washing up the breakfast bowls, he said, "I really like your dad, Ellie. Why would you or your mother leave him?"

"She always said she'd leave when I grew up," Ellie said.

"What was the matter? He doesn't seem like the kind of man who'd hassle you."

"Oh, he's more mellow now," Ellie said.

They left Houston in a hurry because Abe wandered into the neighbor's yard and looked in the sliding glass patio door before his overalls were out of the dryer. Halfway to Galveston they discovered Jerry had two bottles of Ellie's father's Scotch.

"That's stealing," Paul said angrily.

"He saw them," Jerry replied. "He didn't care. He had a whole case."

Paul remembered tears in the tall man's eyes when Ellie kissed him on the cheek and said, " 'Bye, Daddy." Maybe Jerry was right. It wasn't the Scotch he cared about losing.

Paul drove south with Cat and Sid beside him. "I still don't see why you protect Jerry," he said. "He's always getting us in trouble. You don't believe in liquor."

"He saved my life," Cat said. "It's that simple."

"Peace and brotherhood," Sid intoned. "The simple magic of freedom. Besides, he can't help himself. He knows it. He depends on us."

Paul gripped the wheel. Could he depend on them too? he wondered. Nothing was clear.

In Victoria Johanna found a sale of green flowered cotton for ten cents a yard and bought the bolt. She and Ellie sewed all the way across Texas.

Somewhere in the Valley between Port Isabel and McAllen behind a palm-bordered orange grove on the dike beside the Rio Grande, Johanna had a bad trip and danced all night. For Johanna that wasn't unusual except that she wasn't singing "hidy ho," she was screaming. They picked oranges and squeezed the juice down her throat. Fresh orange juice, they'd heard, was the best antidote. Abe held her tight till the sun came up and wouldn't let her lie down. Only Abe was strong enough to keep Johanna on her feet when she wanted to fall. Paul wondered what the Mexican farm workers thought of the green-flowered madwoman screeching to the starry skies all night. In the morning he helped Abe swim her in the wide river.

They drove along the highway near the Rio Grande, through countless hours in the King Ranch, through tiny hamlets where barefoot children stared as their truck in tow passed through. They swam near Vulcan Dam. They spent a night in Laredo. They followed the river toward its source all the way to Big Bend.

When Paul saw the sun rise over the red canyon rim, he reached for his camera. It wasn't with his mess kit. It wasn't anywhere. He felt like crying. Dad, he said, somebody stole the camera you gave me.

He called home collect and asked Jojo to phone the insurance company. "They should pay a couple of hundred dollars for it," he said.

131

Jojo sounded excited. "Where are you?" he asked. "It's been months since you called."

Paul looked at the stark red stone bluffs against the blistering sky. "In the desert. I got out of the van to pee, and when I got back, the camera was gone."

"Never mind the camera. Where are you? What will I tell your mother?"

"Dad gave it to me. I'm sure the insurance company—"

"You're crazy. Don't you know where you are?"

Paul looked at Amy waiting outside the phone booth. "That's a relative question," he said. "Where you are depends on where you want to be. Everything is relative."

"How'd it go?" Amy asked when he hung up.

"Not too bad, relatively speaking," Paul said.

They drove to a town high in the mountains near Taos and could see peaks even higher. "Someday I'll get to the top of one of those," Paul said. He couldn't remember why.

Amy nodded. "Me too. In the summer, when it's warmer. You get to the top of one of those, and it'd be like touching God."

"Or your father," Paul said.

In the desert in Arizona he watched Ellie brush her hair again and said he wanted to touch it. Ellie wrapped him in her long corn-silk hair. They sat among the cacti and watched two lizards play. Paul touched her hair and her beautiful smooth cheek. He touched her lips with his finger and then with his lips, but he didn't say he loved Ellie and she didn't ask.

He wondered how he could have made love to two women when he didn't love either one. He wondered why he called what they did "making love."

"Do we love each other?" he asked her.

"Love is irrelevant," she said.

He watched a spiny lizard cross the sand. "What do you mean?"

"It's nice to be touched. It feels so nice. It doesn't have anything to do with love."

"So you don't love me." He was hurt.

"I love everyone," Ellie said gently. "Of course I love you." Then she brushed his straw hair until his whole body tingled like swimming in soda. And with her wonderful quick fingers she braided his straw to her corn silk and for a crazy while they were one. They couldn't stop laughing when they got up to walk back to camp with their heads together; they fed each other hot bean enchiladas with their fingers and licked the drippings off their burning lips.

In Arizona Cat stood on a rock at the dinner meeting. She placed Sid's hand on her stomach. "Our baby is as big as the head of a pin," Cat said.

"Hidy ho," said Johanna. "Let the tyke grow."

The sun wheeled and the moon grew fat and waned. Paul didn't count the days or the hands or the people who came and stayed or looked and shied away. He didn't count the concrete-floored foul-smelling jails he slept in, the pools of urine, the stench, the roaches, the spiders that he crushed or brushed away. He lost count of the nightmares that stirred his sleep, or the bong . . . bong . . . of the mournful bell that penetrated his brain, calling him, reproaching him.

They sold the pickup and the bucket of parts when they ran out of the long green. "We'll get another bus in California," Sid said. "We'll pick some lettuce and have another festival. This time without the cops-and-robbers scene. That old pickup never did run right."

They were out of everything but pot, which Amy was growing in a dresser drawer she'd found at a town dump. So they sold the steering wheel for some hash and went on to California. Sid said he knew a beach where they could be perfectly free.

"Paradise is near," Amy said.

At the California border Cat stopped the van. She

stretched her arms to the sky. "Our baby is as big as a pea," she said.

They camped at the foot of one of the great high cliffs overlooking the Pacific Ocean. Sometimes they ate fish, and sometimes vegetables, but mostly beans. Paul got used to the hollow-bellied feeling when they ran low. One or another of them would hire out to a local farm in picking season. Their family grew or shrank depending on visitors.

One day Paul borrowed a motorcycle and drove with Ellie hanging on to him all the way to Riverside to find Joe.

At first Joe didn't recognize him, and barred his way outside the second-floor apartment.

Dumb, Paul waited for Joe to say something, reach in his pocket for a bill, send him away, anything.

"What the hell," Joe exploded when he finally caught on. "What have you done to yourself?"

"This is Ellie. Can we come in?"

Joe opened the door reluctantly. "You should have called. I didn't know you were in town. I've got a six-hour qualifying exam in the morning and—"

"That's okay," Paul said. "We won't stay long. How's it going?"

"Does Mom know you're here? Last time she wrote—"

"No."

Joe shook his head. "Let's call her."

"Maybe later." Paul sat down.

"You want to shower up? Shave?" Joe took off his heavy-rimmed glasses and rubbed his eyes.

"No, thanks." Paul let his hands hang between his knees. He thought Joe didn't want him touching anything. "You got anything to eat?"

"Not much." Joe put some cheese and a couple of pieces of bread on a plate. "I could go to the store, but I planned to eat out."

134

"I don't want you to go to any trouble, Joe." Paul handed Ellie the cheese. They sat in awkward silence.

"Did you always wear those glasses?" Paul asked.

"I got them last summer."

"They make you look different."

Joe wheeled, and his voice was angry. "Damn, I knew you were on the loose. Mom kept calling me, but I didn't see what I could do. I told her not to worry. You'd be okay. But I never thought—"

"I'm not loose. I have the Family." Paul picked up Ellie's hand.

"What the hell." Joe shook his head again. "Have you looked in a mirror recently?"

Paul laughed. "Only the mirror of a quiet pool or a perfect sky. Have you ever thought of the sky as a mirror?" He knew he didn't sound like himself, but this man with the glasses was a stranger.

"Don't tell me about it. Out here there's every kind of loony. Cults, groupies, encounters, hands on, hands off. After Jonestown I don't know how much longer I can stand even living in a state where things like that start."

"Don't worry," Paul said. "The Family isn't didactic. We believe in freedom, love, peace, not blind obedience."

Joe looked up. "Shit." Nodding to Ellie, he said it again. "Last time I saw you was two Christmases ago. You used to be a cute kid, really good. You worked hard, played hard too. You were so cheerful. What happened?"

"Working hard never helped Dad much." Ellie wandered around looking at Joe's books. "This computerized society—"

"Paul, you're out-of-date." Joe began to pace, glancing nervously at Ellie. "When I was your age, it was different. You were too young to understand. There were so many bad things going on, we had to protest. Somehow drugs got mixed up in it too. I don't know how, but they sure never

135

helped. Now the kids who care are studying, working, trying to find better ways to change the world."

"I'm not trying to change anything," Paul said.

"Well, you ought to be. That's your legacy. I blame myself. I should have gone home more."

Ellie said quietly, "We have no space for guilt, Joe. Paul is his own person, perfectly free."

Joe stopped talking, caught, Paul knew, by her utter sincerity. He took off his glasses and rubbed his eyes. "Sorry, kid, you're my brother. It kills me to see you wasted."

Some legacy, Paul thought, remembering an energy bar and a Vuitton trunk full of dead dreams. "I'll study later." He stood up. "Next year. I can go home anytime. I don't see any reason to now, when I have everything I want."

"Yeah." Joe reached into his pocket and came up with a ten-dollar bill. "Buy yourself a meal," he said. "And come back. Call first, though. I'll let Mom know you were here."

"See you later," Paul said.

FOURTEEN

Dandelion was born in the fall, just after the rainy season.
Paul couldn't believe the baby. He'd never seen fingernails so small. Some days he saw Jerry's half-whiskered
face on the little froglike body and some days he saw Sid's
beard. Once, looking in the bright blue eyes, it was like
looking into a mirror. Watching Cat feed Dandelion with
her breast, he said wonderingly, "You a mother! I can't
believe it."

"Not me," Cat said. "Not that trip!"

"But—"

"The sun is the father; the moon the mother; all the
Family are guardian angels," she said. She smiled as if he
wasn't there, and tears coated her cheeks. She looked so
old. Paul remembered the screams that had filled Sid's
tepee the night they all stood around wondering miserably
what to do while Dandelion was getting born.

Through aimless days past counting he combed the
beach for treasures—shells, firewood, and newly stranded
fish. He walked the brown hills with Abe, brooded on the
future of mankind with Sid, sat in a cool pool of foam
among the rocks with Amy, watched the gulls while Ellie
brushed his hair, sat under the lime tree cradling Dandelion
in his arms while Cat read aloud.

But in the aimless days he'd sometimes remember Joe's
cautions and the mountains that now stood between him

137

and his distant past. *I can go home anytime,* he'd told Joe. Could he?

I have everything I want. Then why was he crying? Did he know the way through the continental divide? *Freedom ain't a freedom unless you exercise it,* Sid would say. What did that mean?

One day he found a Dacron line on the beach and tried to remember how to tie a bowline. *Get a book,* he told himself, and tossed the line away.

He watched two sailboats all afternoon, racing each other far offshore. If he studied as hard as Joe, would the nightmares stop?

One day he rode the cycle back to Riverside and walked into the admissions office of the Community College. "I'd like to take some courses," he said to the bright-eyed girl at the desk.

"Which degree?" she asked, and, "Where did you get your high-school diploma?"

"See you later," Paul said, and stumbled out.

Back at camp Ellie hooked his arm. "I missed you all day," she said. Dandelion gurgled with delight and rolled over. Sid said, "You're young and strong and everyone depends on you, Paul. If anything happens to me, you will lead the Family."

But when it rained, it was like the night. Whether calm or stormy, windy or still, the sound of the sea filled Paul's head by day and his dreams by night.

Cat was herself again. "We'll stay in California forever," she said. "The sun follows us, and nights are short."

Two men and a woman on their way to Alaska in an old hearse they'd bought for fifty dollars joined them one afternoon. They sat around the fire late, talking about the pipeline and what life it had brought to the forty-ninth state.

Sid talked of the shame of staining the north slope with

138

oil. Cat said she'd counted forty dead birds after the last oil spill. "Alaska's the future," their visitors said. "There's space for the pipeline and people and wilderness too. There's work and freedom and clean air."

One of the men sat next to Ellie, stroking her arm. "There's room in the hearse if you want to join us," he said, inviting Ellie with his eyes.

"Have you ever been there?" Jerry asked. "Freeze your goddamn balls off." His eyes were burning.

The next morning Ellie was gone and so was the hearse. Had she decided in the middle of the night to go to Alaska? They spread out, searched, and called.

"I heard her get up in the night, but I fell asleep before she came back," Jerry said.

"What time was that?" they asked him, but he didn't know; the moon had gone under, and his watch had stopped months before.

Neither happy nor sad, never impatient or angry, Ellie was as calm and steady as a sun-drenched sea under a southwest wind. She accepted each of them uncritically. She wouldn't desert them. Her pleasure in their company flowed around them, holding them together, soothing, nourishing. Her disappearance this unusually raw March morning made them fearful, sensitive to the wind. They avoided each other's eyes.

Jerry found her at the foot of the cliff lying in a strange position, her braids one way, her legs another. Had she, believing in her immortality, followed a shooting star and flown off that cliff? Had she stumbled in the dark? Had she (they shuddered at the thought) been attacked, frightened, slipped in a struggle, or been pushed? There was no way to know. Death without witness isolated them. They couldn't comfort each other.

They called her father, remembering his mellowness. He flew out and stood wet-eyed among them in an ugly parlor

139

while an organ played dolorous music that she would never have heard. The sound and the smell were not new to Paul. He was a long, long way from home.

They left California when the lime tree was starting to bloom, Ellie's ashes in its shade, where, from that cool grave, the surf music mingled with the cries of gulls.

In Colorado the air was sharp and creeks ran so clear Paul could watch trout among glittering stones. The bright sky was etched with peaks that alternately beckoned and threatened him. In Colorado the nights were longer than the days. West of the continental divide he'd imagined himself strong. What would he be when they crossed over?

One night Abe didn't show up for the dinner meeting. "Don't worry," Sid said. "Abe knows the trail."

But the next night he still wasn't there. Johanna danced so long the little brown ground squirrels stopped twittering and went about their business as usual. She danced all night and sang, and it took both Sid and Paul all their strength to keep her from running into the black night to hunt for Abe. They were camped by a high lake well off the tiny dirt trail of a road that led winding and climbing to their lonely glen. They were surrounded by bare rock peaks, look-alike stands of fluttering aspen and brooding dark green spruce. But there were no orange trees here, no antidote they knew within arm's reach.

They held her tight, and just after dawn, when she began to screech, the ground squirrels sat upright and twittered again. Though Paul and Sid swam Johanna in the lake out past the reeds, her cries became wilder; she fought and thrashed out of her mind. So they piled in the van, Cat drove fast, winding and looping down the dirt road, with Amy holding Dandelion up front and Paul and Sid embracing the screeching Johanna, one on her arms and one on her legs, until they reached the hospital. Jerry guarded the

140

camp. Cat loved everyone, and everyone included Jerry, but she never left Dandelion alone with him.

Amy quoted Keats all the way up the beautiful winding trail. They couldn't get lost. Up was where they were going; down was home.

Paul inhaled deeply. "I knew it would be like this. Clean air and a trail to the top of the world."

"I'm hot," Amy said. "Let's stop for a drink."

They splashed their faces in a fast-running creek and Paul filled his canteen. The trail left the creek and wound around the side of the mountain. The higher they climbed, the shorter their breath, the heavier Paul's pack. Sunlight flickered through the towering spruce.

"The tree line is near," Paul said.

"I'm hungry," said Amy.

They found a well-sheltered rock ledge where they ate some of their raisins and a bag of nuts. "Let's spend the night here," Paul said, dropping his pack. They stripped to their T-shirts and shorts, leaving everything else on the ledge, and went on.

Above the tree line the sun beat down and their throats parched.

The trail crossed a dry meadow studded with rocks and wildflowers. Around an uplift of granite the narrowing path spiraled ever steeper. They clung to the rock wall to keep from slipping off the precipice. A fresh breeze came up. Paul rubbed his bare arms.

They inched around the crag. The wind blew harder. They crawled. It was as frightening as it was beautiful, but they couldn't turn back.

They knew they had touched the sky because they felt it everywhere. They knew they were in heaven because they were above the clouds and there was nowhere up to go.

"Beauty is truth, truth beauty,—that is all/ Ye know on

141

earth, and all ye need to know," quoted Amy. "I wish Ellie were here. She always wanted to touch the sky, to fly. *Thou wast not born for death, immortal bird."*

It was the first time anyone had said her name since they left California. He saw her suddenly, her braids pointing like an arrow to her heart. He couldn't speak.

Though the wind tried to pluck them off, they stayed on that point of rock awhile, watching birds below and shadows of other mountains move across the valley. They shared a joint and made up stories about the shapes of the shadows. The wind turned cold.

"Let's go," Amy said, "I'm freezing."

They picked their way down, bruising their fingers on the rough granite. It was harder descending. Paul tested with his toe each stone or stretch of gravel for safe footing.

"I don't like looking down," Amy said. "It's so black."

"If we can just reach the meadow before it gets dark it will be easier." Paul's words hung in the void. *It was dark now.*

How many hours had they climbed since noon? How far down were their sleeping bags, their supper, their long-sleeved shirts, their matches? They had no idea.

Suddenly Paul couldn't see where to put his foot. He grabbed Amy's arm. They stood motionless. He let his head fall back, as stunned by the star-studded canopy above as by the black chasm below. Terrified, he thought, Hansel and Gretel without crumbs. He dropped to the ground, pulling Amy down beside him.

"Are we lost? I'm hungry. Have we anything left to eat?"

He laughed. He loved her. Who better to be lost at the top of the world with than Amy. "You never told me your last name," he said.

She pushed against him for warmth. "Look," he said. "Each star had a baby since last night. Dandelions everywhere but no mother, no moon. You can't read by starlight except what the stars themselves have written."

"Keep talking," she said, "your voice rumbles inside me and keeps me warm. So long as you talk, I know I'm alive." Everywhere they didn't touch the cold painted them. He clung to Amy and to consciousness. He talked; he tried to read the stars. Now and then he slipped off and met the nightmares. Between dreams the stars arced over his head but he couldn't read what they said, Vega or Polaris, or Sirius or . . .

"I've forgotten how to read," he wept. "I've forgotten everything I knew."

In my day a fellow didn't walk out on his responsibilities. It's your legacy.

His arm cradled Amy's head. Pebbles dug holes in his flesh. Forcing his eyes open, he explained how all the stars wheeled around the North Star. His eyes were his camera, closing and opening their shutters. When he developed the film in the morning each star would be a white curve on the film. When Mary Lou saw the film she wouldn't mind being out so late. *Nobody cares where you go or what you do.*

Orion sleeps under the sea in July and August, but don't worry. He won't drown. He has a lifeline to a star. If you want to know where you are, just find the North Star and point your camera eyes. Blink. Open the shutters.

It was gone. Polaris was hiding. Follow the cup of the Big Dipper, dumdum. Liar! The North Star was gone, ruining his film, fogging his lenses. Hiding behind the sails like a criminal, he heard the mournful bell. *Ready about!* But he lost the tiller and he lost the sheet. The boom slammed over and the sail flapped free. Someone cried. He tried to wipe his eyes but the boom pinned his arm. *Betelgeuse. Bastard.*

This the boy, sir?

Hold him . . . jail him . . .

You'll have to bring charges . . .

He was frozen in jail, ice-bound, encased, entombed. His icicle fingers would snap if he bent them. See the frozen blood in the broken ends. See the frozen pump in his freezing heart. Don't move, you're brittle. Don't move, you'll break. Don't blink. Don't breathe. Don't.

"Don't cry," Paul said to Amy, "or your tears will freeze." That first streak of sunlight hit his eyelids so suddenly, dazzling him with its glare. He brushed snow from her face and neck. "I once read a story by Jack London. So long as we stay dry we'll be all right."

Her eyes were dark circles. Her lips quivered. But then, "*Fled is that music: —Do I wake or sleep?*"

The ground was dark where they had slept. Everything else was white except Amy's lips, which were blue. She started to stand.

Paul put out his arm. "Careful." Then pointing down, "Look."

She peered past his shoulder. There was nothing below for hundreds of feet, then rubble, then the tops of some spruce poked through a thick cloud. It was dawn here, but still night below. They were on an overhang.

"It's good you don't thrash around in your sleep," Amy said. "How come it's so cold? It was summer yesterday."

"The air's thinner up high, so there's less of it to hold the heat of the sun."

"How come you know so much?"

"I don't remember how I know that. Someone probably told me." Then he added, "Maybe I learned it in school."

"I doubt it," Amy said.

"There are lots of things I don't remember," Paul said suddenly. "The trouble is, I don't know what they are."

"Don't worry," Amy said. "Just so you know who you are."

When they reached the aspen at the edge of camp, they heard music. The Family had company. Dandelion toddled happily among the strangers.

Paul stopped. "Do me a favor, Amy. Take Dandelion for a walk today."

"I've had enough."

"Please."

Amy looked perplexed.

Paul explained, "She cried when I left yesterday because I wouldn't take her. I promised a walk today."

"Well?"

"I don't want to break my promise, but I won't be here. . . . I'm going home, Amy," he went on. "Back to Rocky Shores. Tell them. Tell Sid and Cat for me at the dinner meeting. I'm not ready to die or disappear. I'm too young to walk off a cliff. I don't remember who I am."

"Pleasure never is at home," Amy said.

"Pleasure?"

"But you said—"

"I made a mistake."

They watched Sid grab Dandelion and toss her squealing into the air. Paul wondered where she would be ten years from now. He tried not to cry.

"That's okay," Amy said finally. "Lots of people make mistakes. Just be careful. Don't phone."

Suddenly he said, "Come with me. Together we'll make it. We never did find your paradise anyway."

She shook her head. "No. I'm nearer paradise than you think." Her feet began to move in time to the music.

Paul tilted her chin up, trying to memorize her pretty, puffy face, all lips and eyes in a puddle of black hair. He kissed her lips. "I love you, Amy. I probably always will."

"Life is but a day; A fragile dewdrop . . ."

Later he thought: Wherever she is, Amy will make her own paradise.

And still later he wondered: Can I?

145

I can't get over the girl who died. The one with the braids. No wonder you get sad. I wonder if you loved her. I don't understand what you said: "I don't know. She loved everyone. Not just me." But you didn't say anything about how you felt. I'd like to hear you laugh. Joke!

This boat is really moving. I'd forgotten how great it feels when we go fast.

Today I think I am the daring one. Today I feel as if the sky belongs to me and I am the sky. You came home. You are here. Getting to know you all over again is the most glorious thing that has happened to me in my life.

I could fly.

FIFTEEN

He didn't know how long he'd been sitting on the bed when he heard the key in the front-door lock. He'd never been away. He'd been away forever. He gripped the ribbed cotton spread. His blue bedspread. Everything in this room was his. The books were his books. The half-finished half-hull was his. The racing chart pinned to the wall, his chart. He'd never won a trophy. The room was a stage set, a boy's room. He'd walked onto the stage, sat down, but the director was missing, he was miscast.

Just so you know who you are.

The front door opened, thump, closed. The ship's clock chimed. Her footsteps crossed the hall. He heard paper-bag sounds from the kitchen, saw Cat pulling out beans, salt, matches. He put his hands over his ears. He mustn't cry.

Footsteps crossed the hall again. The closet door opened, hangers rattled, door shut. He looked out the window. Heavy summer foliage, dripping from the afternoon rain, blocked any view.

Footsteps mounted the stairs, stopped, continued. Tired steps, he thought, end-of-a-long-day steps. The clock by the bed said 12:45. But the digits didn't change. He visualized neat blue shoes on each tread, on the landing. Still he waited.

"Oh ... My ... God."

147

He let her hug him. He held her up, this strange small woman, because she would have fallen. With her arms around him, he half-remembered her. But it was like being hugged by a distant aunt. *Kiss Aunt Lizzie, Paul.* He moved his chin so his face only brushed hers. He stood quite still while this strange-smelling woman—half-transparent skin stretched over high cheekbones—tried to put her old lips on his cheek. A strange aunt. *She* didn't have old lips.

She was so much smaller than he remembered, thinner, bonier, smaller than Cat. Somebody's mother. He was in one of the nightmares that he couldn't wake from. He had to go all the way through, live everything, before it would be over. There was no shortcut. No waking. No dream. He was home.

"Why didn't you phone? When did you get here? How did you get in? Let me look at you!"

He let go and she nearly fell, but regained her balance and tried to master herself.

"Those sores on your legs, Paul, how did you get them? Those shorts—you're falling out of them. Where's your laundry? You must have laundry. When did you last have a bath? Dr. Arnold better look at your legs. Take a shower. You need a shave. You didn't even need to shave when you left. Put on something clean. Do you have a razor? Your clothes are in the closet. I'll phone—"

"Did you buy any milk?" he interrupted her.

"How stupid of me. You're hungry. Of course. Yes, I brought some in with me. I'll call Jojo. He's down at the Yacht Club in the afternoons now. He'll want to know you're home. And Joe too. We'll phone him. He called me after you were there. He told me about the girl. Is she—?"

"Careful," he said. "Don't phone."

"Why not? What's the matter with phoning?"

He couldn't tell her. He didn't know her, or himself either. If he told her anything, he'd tell too much.

She was still talking. Talking, he remembered, was what she did instead of crying. His father told him that once. "When your mother talks a lot, she does that to keep from crying." But after he died, anything made her cry and she didn't talk so much. That was a long time ago.

She was talking when he got in the shower, and on the phone when he got out. As he came downstairs, wearing his old yellow oxford shirt, she started again. He couldn't button the shirt, and the sleeves hardly came past his elbows. She stopped when she saw he still wore his torn dirty shorts.

Then: "You've got hair on your chest. Your hair. When did you last have it cut? I made an appointment with Dr.—"

"Don't make appointments for me," he said before he thought. "My sores are not your business now."

"Oh!" She stared, then turned away. He felt her hurt but couldn't do anything about it. He had no connection with her. Miscast; her house was not his stage. He couldn't let her wrap him, direct his play, worm her way inside him, eat his insides; not if he wanted to stay.

And he wanted to, just for a while. He thought of the clean sheets under that blue spread. One night with a white-cased pillow under his head—he wanted that.

"Are any of Joe's or Dad's clothes around I could wear till I can get some for myself? Nothing fits."

"I don't know." She tried to be distant, dignified. "I'll look."

When he finished the eggs and bacon she fried for him, he put his hands on the table. "Thanks. That was good." He had to give her something. That was safe. He didn't want to tell her how long since he'd sat at a table to eat.

She nodded cautiously, acknowledging the gesture. But she didn't talk anymore. He was sorry. He felt her unasked questions all around him. Talking was better than crying, but crying would be better than the silence. He felt her concern, lead weights on his shoulders. The thick atmosphere suffocated him. He couldn't stay. He shouldn't have tried to come back until he was stronger. If you were a burden, a disappointment, a failure, it was easier not to see the people you had failed.

"Can I stay here a couple of days till I find a place?"

It turned into more than a couple.

They made a deal. They said he could live at home, eat and sleep there, if he went to school. There was still time to register for the fall term. If he didn't go to school, he'd have to contribute to the support of the house, pay rent and board and help with the chores. He'd agreed, but he didn't love it. Conditions were everywhere.

His first job lasted two days, the next one five. Finally he was hired as a delivery boy for a garage. He said he'd had experience as a mechanic in the west. He'd worked on carburetors. He still had his driver's license. He parked the car he was delivering in a side lot and went to pick up some parts. The place was crowded and slow as usual; the men behind the counter took their time in the stock room, looking up prices and numbers in their thick catalogs. By the time his turn came, he couldn't remember the parts he was supposed to buy. He phoned the shop. The service manager —his boss—yelled into the phone. Why was he taking so long? The customer had called and was waiting for his car. Paul left the car at the auto-parts shop and walked down to the boatyard. He didn't need to be yelled at. He hadn't walked and crawled halfway across the continent for that.

So he lost two days' pay. He bought a quart of ice cream and a paper and went home. He was eating and reading the ads when Jojo came in.

"I thought you'd be working," Jojo said.

"I was." Paul didn't look up from the paper.

"Um. Two-thirty's pretty early to be home, isn't it?"

"Nope," Paul said.

150

"They paying you by the hour? Can't make enough to keep a chicken alive in these times if you quit at two-thirty."

"That was a lousy job," Paul said. "I'm looking for something. There are a couple of leads here."

"Jobs are scarce. You were lucky to get anything." Jojo was quiet a moment. Then: "Your mother said you'd pay your way. I don't reckon fifty percent of nothing's going to get her far."

Paul stood up. He was taller than Jojo, stronger. Jojo looked so old, too old to get mad at. Paul held himself in, but he didn't like the feeling.

"I thought I'd go down to the boatyards and see if they need any help. Who'd you say you knew down there?"

"I told you his name yesterday. George Pritchard. His son's studying mapmaking. George might put you in training if he likes you. Give you a chance to learn the business from the bottom up. Navigation. Design. Construction. Sales. Weather. George knows it all. He'd let you work part-time in the factory, go to school part-time. If you worked hard and he liked you, he'd treat you like a son. Liked your dad a whole lot too. Once wanted him to go into partnership—"

"What'd you say his name was?"

Jojo scratched his head. "I just told you!"

"I know, but then you got talking and I forgot."

Jojo's white eyebrows hit his white hair. His eyes looked scared. "So quick?"

Paul shrugged. He didn't answer right away. He didn't want his voice to show how hard his heart was banging. He didn't know how he forgot so quick. He forgot a lot of things. He never knew what he would remember, what he'd forget. He only knew he didn't have control of his own mind, though he hadn't smoked dope in a month. Like forgetting what he was supposed to buy. Or on that job he had a week ago, cooking french fries in a hamburger place, how hot the fat was supposed to be. Or how many orders he'd filled. Or the job the week before as a carpenter's helper, what size nail he was told to use, where he was supposed to hammer the two-by-four crosspieces on the stairs he was supposed to know how to build. So for a minute he pretended to be cool, and finally when his heart slowed down, he said, "Oh, well, never mind. It doesn't matter. I don't want to go into the boat business anyway."

Who wants to be treated like a son? Not me! Not that trip! "See you later," he said, and started out the door.

"Hey. Where're you off to? You home for dinner? What'll I tell your mother?"

Paul paused. He couldn't help what he said next. Jojo would have to learn not to ask so many questions. "Tell her anything you like." He regretted it instantly. He was too old to hurt Jojo. What was the matter with him? He'd been home a month, and he was hurting them as if he was still a punk kid. In all the time he'd been with the Family, he'd never hurt anyone.

Except when he left. He hadn't stayed to see the hurt, but at least they knew he wasn't dead.

"Sorry, Jojo," he said. "Tell her I won't be home for dinner, okay?"

Jojo nodded, raised his hand, and let it fall. Paul closed the door softly.

He wandered around town for a while with the newspaper in his hand. He had to have a job. He needed his own money, his own place. He couldn't let them channel or steer him. A room of his own needn't cost much. He looked up and saw the "HELP WANTED" sign on the carwash. Who needed a memory to work there?

I wonder what Cold Spring Harbor is like. You made it sound so perfect, like some sort of paradise. But I don't believe anymore that any place is perfect. Maybe that shows I'm growing up. No place has been yet, at least not for me.

How long are you going to wait to kiss me? Are you afraid I'll pull away? I don't think so. I know you're afraid of something. Maybe feeling too much, the way we did before. Like wanting to laugh and cry at the same time. There's a headland. I wonder if that's where we're going. I'm not going to ask. No one but you ever made me want to cry. Not Reggie or Roy or any of the others I went out with.

I can't wait to get where we're going—I don't care where. Anywhere!—but I could keep sailing like this forever.

SIXTEEN

"What did your mother say when she first saw you?" Mary Lou asked. They'd anchored, had a swim, eaten enough supper to be content, and now lay on the foredeck watching the pink glow make its way up the sky. The water of the harbor was a blue sheet. When they didn't speak, they heard fish break the surface, birds on the low hills ask pert questions, gulls cry critical comments. Swallows skimmed the surface where evening insects swarmed.

"She said I needed a shave."

"She was probably right."

"Probably."

"Did you then?"

"What?"

"Shave."

"No, not then."

"Why?"

"I shave when I want to."

"That's the way it is for me too."

"You shave?" He stroked her smooth cheek.

She laughed. "Oh, you know."

"No."

"I mean, I don't want them telling me when to do things. I know what I have to do and what I want to do."

"What do you want to do?" He watched a gull dive and rise with a fish in its beak.

"I want to travel, to see the places you've seen. I do want to go to California, to see another ocean. I like knowing people from other places. Sometimes I think with horror: What if I'd never left Texas! I don't want to hear any more about what nice girls do or don't do. How do they know? They don't know anything about what I think or do."

Resting on his elbow, he watched her, tried to imagine her in California, Arizona, Colorado. Green-flowered or naked in a creek. He couldn't. She was orange-striped and never braided her hair.

"That wouldn't work out," he said. "I wouldn't want you to be where I've been."

"Why?"

"You're too young."

"Oh!" He'd insulted her. She bit her lip. Then she said, "No, I'm not a kid. I don't feel like one. You're not the only one of us who's had experiences."

"I know that, but . . ." He didn't know how he wanted to phrase the question. He didn't know if he wanted the answer.

"Would it make any difference to you if I said there were six good smokes in my ditty bag?" she asked slowly.

He wasn't surprised, but he had trouble with the idea, too. "That's a lot of pot for one person to smoke all by herself."

"I meant to share."

"I know. Of course." There was so much he wanted to explain to her, but he wasn't finding words. She wanted to know everything, to try everything. He wanted her to know how he felt without knowing everything. If he smoked with her, he might tell more than he wanted. Why was everything suddenly difficult? Each word he said mattered so much. He wanted it easy.

155

"Look," he said, "that's great you brought them. But I've been trying to leave it alone. So maybe later, but not now."

"Why? Do you think it hurts you?"

"I don't know. I have this problem of forgetting things. And remembering what I don't want to remember. It's as if somebody else has hold of my mind and won't let go. Sometimes it's okay—like now—and I've got the strings. But I thought I'd leave it alone awhile."

She shrugged. "I can take it or leave it."

"Let's have a swim," he said, "and explore the beach while it's still light. You can decide whether you want to sleep there or on the boat. Tomorrow morning we'll sail into the town and see what it's like. I haven't been there in years."

"Okay."

He didn't know why he hadn't kissed her yet, or that he was half-waiting for her to say, let's sail home.

The water, richly opaque like old velvet, changed so fast it was hard to keep pace—from blue to pink to gray to purple. Except for their breathing, there were no sounds. After dark the birds were still. They walked at the water's edge. The still air was as warm as the water. They could swim out to the boat anytime, and under a rising moon sail home. If they wanted to. If the wind came up as it often did after dark.

They sat with their backs against the dune, wrapped in their separate thoughts, wrapped in the charged air. Now and then a word passed, but long silences held them as tightly to each other as words. Their thoughts were uncontrolled, though they never did have a smoke.

He held her shoulder against his, stroking her arm with his fingertips. She hugged her own knees, held them tight together as if her arms were cords.

After a long time he said, "I think I still love you, Mary

156

Lou." He had to say that first. He took her chin and turned her head. He kissed her so gently, lightly, she thought she couldn't stand it.

"Oh!" she said. "Oh!" The word escaped her. She was trying so hard not to throw her weight against him. "Oh!"

"May I?" he murmured against her lips, still brushing them too lightly. And the words made her cry out suddenly, because she heard another voice (Roy's) another time say, with lips that had touched hers lightly, temptingly, but so planned and carefully, that other voice saying, *May I enter you? What are you saving yourself for?* a whining record that she wished she could turn off, not have any memory of to spoil this night, this time.

She shook her head, sobbing, "Don't ask!" Her hair slapped his face, hurting him with her memory, her misery. His arms fell away from her. Unable to help herself, she flung herself against him so that, misunderstanding, he pressed her hip hard, so she felt what she hadn't dared to feel, and he kissed her, thank God, not lightly. He turned her flat on the sand bed, pressed the heaviness of his leg across her until, suddenly, she was touched.

She cried out and dug sharp nails into his back, arching her back so he knew no one had been there before him. Later she lay with her cheek against his chest, and he felt her breath gradually slow and become even.

Then he wept.

This the boy, sir?

Do you want your daughter examined for rape?

While he wept, she slept. And while she slept, he stroked the place on her forehead where the fine blond hairs began.

When I woke, your face was wet. At first I thought it was raining. Then I realized if it was rain I'd be wet too. The only other time I saw a man cry was when Danny was

157

stoned out of his mind one night and thought Barb had died. He kept crying and crying. It was scary. She was right there, but he couldn't see her. It wasn't scary seeing tears on your face, it was awesome. Some moments I feel so close to you, then other moments, like seeing those tears, I feel so distant. I wonder if you'll ever tell me everything. I wonder how many women you've slept with.

I don't care.

I'm glad I said no to Roy now. I never knew I was going to say no. Barb thought I was crazy to keep taking the pill and not sleeping with anyone. I am scared about having a baby. Even though I took the pill, I'm still scared. How can one little pill do anything?

I don't know what I'd do with a baby. Even your baby. Not yet.

I wish I knew why you were crying.

You used to laugh your way out of everything. I'd get so mad at you for laughing when I was crying. Now I can't cry anymore and you've got tears all over your cheeks. I'll bet you don't want me to notice.

Maybe you do. I wish I had a smoke. I haven't told you how much I like to smoke. All by myself. Not with other boys. Maybe I don't want you to know. I wish I could tell you how I feel this morning. It isn't morning, though.

I lost control of myself. Just like Daddy said girls did. I wasn't even high. Being angry is a little like being high. You lose control. That's why I wouldn't smoke with Roy. I knew I'd lose control. Once you let somebody do something, you can't ever let them not do it.

Like kissing.

Like your putting yourself into me.

But it wasn't like that. I didn't let you do it, I made you do it. I wanted you to. How could I have acted like that? What would my father do if he knew? How can you like me again? Love me? Paul? Are you ashamed of me now?

Paul, will you stop crying and look at me now that the moon is out? No black-sky blanket to cover me. Paul?

I wasn't afraid. Only now I'm a little afraid. I'm afraid Barb's doctor's pill won't work.

I keep telling myself that I should be glad the first time is over. That if Daddy only knew, it would serve him right. But I'm not glad and I'm not sorry, and it doesn't have anything to do with Daddy. Or maybe I'm glad and I'm sorry. Once you do it, you can't not have done it. You can't change your mind in the morning and say: Now, see, I really didn't do that after all. Which is the true way I feel? I wish I knew. Or maybe it doesn't matter. Maybe as Roy said: Just live. Don't think so much about it. Take things as they come and enjoy them. That's what I'll do. I'll just take things—I'll take you, Paul, as you are, and enjoy you.

All that matters is you. You're home. You're here. You said you loved me. You've got scabs on your legs, but I won't ask who you got in a fight with. You never were one to fight, no matter what horrible name someone called you. It does serve him right! I wish we could do it again.

The absolutely incredible thing is, now I know. I've done what Barb and Danny, Roy, even my own mother and father have done. I wish I had a mirror. Am I different? I'm still so hot down there! I do feel different. Full. Old. Thrilled. Will everyone looking at me see that you have been inside me? How could they not see?

I think you're asleep now. Look at your hand. It's just flopped there, so warm and heavy on my stomach, careless. That's the one that pulled my orange suit off. That touched me. It's a nice hand, yours.

What will Barb say when she finds out I've gone? I think you really do mean to take me away. At least another night. Or a week. At least a week on Block Island sounds great. I remember everything you've told me about it.

Maybe I'll call Barb tomorrow and get her to lie for me

and say I'm at her house all week. Then I can have more
time to decide what I want to do.
Do I dare run away?
I dare! I dare!
Why are you crying, Paul?
Poor Mom.
I just remembered—I promised her I'd take Jamie to the
zoo next week. Poor Mom. What will Daddy do to her
when he finds out I've gone?

He watched her wake up, put her hand between her legs,
and pull it away quickly. She ran her finger over his
knuckle and in the valleys between his fingers. He couldn't
keep his hand still. It had a life and a will of its own. It
stirred and turned, and then, as if remembering who it was,
moved over her belly, smoothing it so that now her fingers
stayed with it entwined wherever it went. He felt her lifted
again, and she couldn't keep still under that hand, under
him. This time nothing was sudden, but slow, and neither
of them said a word.

When a cloud slipped over the moon, diffusing its white
light, Paul said, "I didn't mean that to happen again."

"Oh?" She caught her breath. "Please don't go away."
Then she said, "Why were you crying?"

"It's a long story." He couldn't go on.

"I'm not sleepy." She tucked her head into his neck and
brushed sand away from his eye. "I could listen all night."

"I should have taken you home, and now it's too late.
That's part of it."

"Tell me the rest."

He did the best he could.

Sometime before the birds awoke she said, "You are the
only person I won't keep secrets from. You're going to
have to know everything."

SEVENTEEN

Once more Paul tucked the tiller under his arm and felt the good breeze freshen. As they crossed the wide harbor toward the break in the hills marking the channel to the little town, he smiled. Mary Lou smiled back. He checked her hold on the jib sheet, then the luff of the sail.

"You're still good crew," he said, putting his free arm around her shoulder.

"Thanks."

They'd lived a lifetime since the morning before. There were still unknowns between them, but not so many mysteries. He saw the excitement in her eyes, glistening as brightly as the water. The bluffs lay like a line of tawny rabbits sleeping on the white sand shores, furry backs ruffled by winds that played across the quiet harbor. It had been a safe, placid, incredibly beautiful place to spend their first night together, to explore their separate lives, their memories. They had stayed on the beach till dawn, swum lazily back to the boat, watched the mist rise off the glass and be caught in the sun's first pale rays. They'd heard the first gull call.

Now, he thought, she looked like a kid on her way to a party. He saw no ravages of a night without sleep. Once they began to talk, they hadn't been able to stop, any more than once they began to make love had they been able to stop. This thirst for love, for sex, for talk, was nowhere near quenched. It would, he thought with the first stirrings of peace inside himself, take a lifetime to satisfy.

"I feel as if I've known you forever. And that I've hardly begun to know you."

"There isn't any hurry, is there?" she teased him.

"Hurry about what?"

"Getting to know me. I mean, don't we have lots of time?"

He put his hand on hers, held it tight a moment. She was right. If they stayed together, there was no hurry. That's what she said she wanted. She dared. "Lots of my friends are living with someone," she said. "I think it would be fun."

He thought of Amy and Cat and, of course, Ellie. He had never judged them, but he'd never put Mary Lou with them.

What had held him so long was that they'd moved with the grace of people who are the same inside as out. But too many connections were missing. More than the comforts of a solid roof or a bed with clean sheets. Home, life, had to be more than the physical arrangements. Had it something to do with the legacy Joe talked about?

"We can both work and find a nice place to live," Mary Lou planned. "We can even live on the boat until—"

"The boat is Jojo's," he reminded her.

"We're just borrowing it," she said.

Last night it had seemed possible. Certainly he knew how to exist on his own. But he had changed during the long night. He had changed her. You weren't the same after sex as before. You never go back. He no longer regretted what had happened, but responsibility weighed on him. Drifting, making decisions for himself was one thing. But now whatever he decided or did involved Mary Lou.

He thought of the sex. Different than it had ever been for

162

him. Not sex, he thought, love. That's what made the difference. *Love is irrelevant. It's nice to be touched.* Pleasure is all right, he thought, but love is nicer. He wasn't ready to sort it all out yet, but he began to feel more confident. If they went off together, it wasn't running away, not the way he had before, escaping in anger and fear. No, this was the beginning of a life together.

"All right," he said, "when we get out of town, we'll head east and see how far the wind takes us."

"That's the most romantic thing I ever heard. I hope it's far."

They strolled hand in hand through the harbor town, looking in shop windows. Everything delighted Mary Lou, the junk jewelry, the shells, the beach clothes. Suddenly he wanted to give her something.

"Come." He pulled her into a store decorated with nets and lobster pots. They had a case of scrimshaw, hand-carved whalebone. He knew it had to be fake, but it was pretty anyway.

"How about this?" He picked out a ring, a single narrow band intricately carved. She tried it on. Her eyes shone gaudily. "I love it!" She held her hand out in front of her.

He spent his next-to-last five-dollar bill, thinking, two hours of french-frying was all it took to make her happy. It had been easy to earn the five bucks. He could do that again anytime.

She turned the ring over and over on her finger.

"Hasn't anyone ever bought you a present?"

Suddenly serious, she said, "You haven't."

Just before they were ready to go back to the boat, he said, "Maybe you should call your mother. Do you want to?"

She stiffened. Her skin became opaque. The shine left her eyes. She raised her chin. "Do you want to call yours?"

163

Her voice sounded like hitting two wooden sticks together. He wanted to hear it musical again.

"I keep forgetting you've grown up," he said.

She walked into the grocery store to the bread rack marked "Supersavers—Day Old." She put a bag in his hand. "Here." He held a dozen beat-up, stale old rolls. He laughed, and her eyes glistened like the water again.

Paul studied the chart on the dock before they took off. Smithtown by noon would be easy with this wind. Between Smithtown, Stony Brook, and Port Jefferson, there was no safe harbor until the tip of Long Island. They'd have an afternoon at Smithtown and start early the next morning for Orient Point.

When they were well past the moorings, he saw white-caps beyond the channel. "Take the helm," he said. "I'll switch to the storm jib. There's no hurry, so we might as well relax."

Even in the protected waters there was enough wave so he had to watch his footing while he changed the sails, stowed the big genoa jib in the cuddy, and raised the small white triangle.

He came aft and took the tiller. Mary Lou looped the jib sheet an extra turn around the winch, but even so Paul had to help her pull it in.

"You'll have to build up those muscles," he said. "I can't have a twenty-pound weakling for a first mate."

"I like that idea of being a first mate." The wind came right off the land, and even with the small jib they ran out of the harbor so fast they were surprised how quickly they faced the open Sound.

"I hate to leave it behind," Mary Lou said. "Will other harbors be so beautiful?" She slipped her arms into the sleeves of her lightweight parka.

"Every harbor has its own atmosphere," he said. "Like every home, I guess."

164

They watched the line of rocks off the point go by. "It would be pretty hard tacking back into Cold Spring today, wouldn't it?"

"Um," he said. Then thought: It's hard going back home when you've been away. Should he tell her? Did she know that already? When he knew they were well clear of the shoals, he pulled in the main and set a more easterly course that would take them on a reach up to Port Jefferson, on the far side of Smithtown Bay.

"With this wind," he said, "we'll be in Smithtown Bay in time for a swim before lunch. If you still want to go. It's hard, you know, going home again once you've left."

"I know," she said, her voice so low he hardly heard her. "But it would serve *him* right if I never went home."

They didn't make it by lunch because the wind didn't hold. So they ate some cheese, lounged, and enjoyed the rising heat. Paul didn't bother to change the jib. They still had plenty of time to reach a safe anchorage before night.

After lunch they were both sleepy. The long night finally caught up with them, they said. Mary Lou offered Paul a joint, but again he refused.

"You go ahead," he said. "I'll sail while you float. I really don't want to. One of us has to keep his wits together."

He leaned against the transom, keeping a light hand on the tiller. He cleated the sheets, as the wind was barely five knots now. Mary Lou settled against him; he hugged her with his knees. He felt her relax. The warmth of her head tucked into his neck stirred him. A child, he thought, trusting and loving. A Dandelion. A snuggler. He stroked her cheek and neck, the swell of her breast, with his free hand. As she settled deeper into her luxurious sleep and closer against him, he wished they were landed right then. No hurry, he thought. There'll be time, and time for loving. He closed his eyes, forced them open again. He mustn't sleep. He mustn't. One of them had to sail.

165

He tried to plan ahead. His mind went around. Their survival depended on his ability to think for two. *You'll lead the Family, Paul, you're young and strong.* Mary Lou wasn't thinking, she was reacting. He'd been there; he knew. He kept hearing her say, *It would serve him right.*

If her father had been different, he thought, they could have each other in Rocky Shores. But Paul wouldn't sneak around. And he dared not suggest an open affair.

He searched the wide water ahead for markers. He searched ahead in time. At the eastern end of the Sound was an island ten miles out at sea. There were things to do there. They could survive. Shelter was easy to arrange on Block Island—permanent population about five hundred. Summer tourists came every day by boat from Providence and Point Judith. He'd sailed with Charley once in the annual Block Island race. In winter there were plenty of empty houses. He could drive a taxi, fix boats, fish, and farm. They wouldn't need much. He scanned the horizon for markers. He was good at picking out a buoy or a tower, watching a shore gradually come clear. Searching ahead in time was harder.

He struggled with notions that weren't easy to arrange in his mind. He pictured himself at a school desk, in a lecture hall. *What degree are you going for?* How could he find out? He saw Joe's dark-rimmed glasses, saw his hand reach into his pocket and find a bill. He saw the incredible look of Mary Lou's tanned stomach, and where the tan stopped. How could he plan? Think? Decide? Do anything if he couldn't stop wanting to make love to her? Pleasure and pain churning in his chest and groin. Would it—could it— go on like this forever?

He thought of a woman with parchment skin stretched tight over high cheekbones saying from a lit doorway, *Did you call, Paul?*

Nothing lasts forever. Not in his life, anyway. People who believed in God could say, "Only God . . ." But he didn't.

Last night had ended though he had wanted it to go on and on. Dawn came. How many rosy dawns like this would there be? He'd wakened in more than one downpour.

His eyes closed; he struggled to open them again. He must not sleep. Mountains, brown rabbits on a close shore, a green-flowered dancer, ground squirrels twittering, an orange-striped swimmer with—suddenly—snow on her face . . . all unbidden pictures in his mind. *How do you learn to control where your mind goes?* He was terribly hot, sweating. He didn't move. He didn't want to wake her. *If he made her go home, would they be separated again? Could he convince her father he was all right so they could be together, at least sometimes? What kind of school, or hospital, would teach his mind to remember the right things, forget the rest? How long would it take?*

The fresh breeze was a relief. He breathed it deep, hugged the tiller which pushed at his elbow, trying to turn the boat off course.

The boom slammed across the boat. They heeled so far over that Paul, seeing water lip over the rail, had that sickening feeling they were going all the way. They fell off the seat. He lost the tiller, knocked the main sheet out of its cleat. The boat righted itself and swung around. Mary Lou sat in the bottom rubbing her hip.

"You okay?" he asked breathlessly.

"I don't know."

"Get the jib if you can." He gripped the tiller again, and hauled in the mainsail, watching the masthead fly, trying to figure where the wind came from.

She uncleated the jib sheet on the port side and let the sail come around, pulling in the starboard sheet and trimming it. "We came about," he said. "I almost fell asleep with you and didn't notice the wind had changed." He stopped and stared down the Sound.

"Look!"

Her eyes followed his, and she gasped. The sudden gust had been only a warning, a scout, for the huge black storm-cloud that touched the water and filled half the sky. It hadn't hit them yet, but it was on its way straight out of the west, coming down the middle of the Sound. It touched both shores. The line of dark, churned-up water in front of it moved steadily toward them.

"Omigod," she said. "What'll we do?"

"Are you all right?" he asked her again.

"I guess so." She was foggy from sleep, from pot too, he guessed. Could he depend on any help from her?

"There are two things to do if you're caught in a storm," he said, thinking out loud, telling himself as much as explaining to Mary Lou. "Run before it until it blows itself out. The sailing can be easier because you're going in the same direction as the wind, but the storm can take longer to pass over you, because you're traveling with it. Or you can beat it, heading into the wind, and hope you can keep moving, keep control, even if you don't make much headway. That way, going against or into the storm, it will pass more quickly and you hope you'll stay clear of any hazards, and stay well offshore.

"If you run before it and the winds are too big, or you're afraid of being blown farther than you want to go, you can drop a sea anchor. I've never done that, but I've read about how it's done. I don't have one on board, though, and I can't think of how to rig one up.

"The most important thing is to stay offshore and hope there aren't any rocks or shoals in mid-Sound. The other thing is to avoid getting abeam of the waves, on a reach, when waves and wind can conspire together to swamp a boat, even one with three feet of keel down like this."

He was surprised at himself. He didn't know that his well of knowledge would find its way into his mind, and onto his tongue. Now he wondered whether his physical ability, his timing, would begin to match his wit. He would have to make decisions—a whole series of them—swiftly, then find the strength to implement them.

First, which way to go?

"Which is easier?" Mary Lou asked in a small, scared voice.

"Neither." He didn't have much time to decide. The dark water approached steadily. "Maybe we could reef the main and blow on out with her. We'd end up somewhere between here and Block Island Sound if we stayed clear of Smithtown Bay."

"Let's do that, since that's where we want to be. Maybe we could get someplace safe before it hits."

"Not a chance." The cloud swelled above his head like a gigantic expanding parachute, rising and blanketing the sky.

"I'll reef the main. Take the helm. Let the sail luff, don't hold her tight, and when I tell you, head up. Hold her into the wind until I make the sail fast."

"Okay."

He went forward, working against time, his fingers remembering how he'd looped and tied the halyard. His mind wrestled with the decision he had to make—a decision, he knew, on which their survival hinged.

If he headed before the storm, would they end up where they needed to be? If he pointed into that black cloud, could he hold the boat against the storm?

"Head up?" he yelled against the gathering wind. There were whitecaps all around them now, and the prow pitched in the choppy water. Mary Lou struggled to hold the sail, keeping the luff in as he had told her. She braced her weight on the tiller, pushing it toward the sail. The sail flapped, and he let it down to the second row of reefing ties, then secured the halyard again. After he tied the little lines around the furled bottom of the sail to the boom, he called back, "Okay, head off a bit."

The sail went on flapping. "Head off," he said, reaching for the tiller.

"I don't know which way is off."

He started to laugh. Amy might have said that. Which way was off? Which way was on? It all depends. But he didn't laugh because rain drove into his face so he couldn't see. The masthead fly spun. Rain hit his eyes. "Loosen the jib," he cried. "Sit in the bottom and hold the sheet as best you can, but don't pull it tight. Can you reach the life jackets?"

The boat spun twice while Mary Lou crawled forward and got the jackets. He had one arm in his and helped her with hers. They sat in the bottom and clung to the sheets.

"Please," she cried, and he didn't know whether he saw tears or rain on her face. "Please, please!"

"Please what?" he screamed back at her.

"Please run!" she screamed. "Don't stay here! Run!"

He gripped her shoulder, but with all his strength held the tiller and pointed the prow of the boat into what he hoped was oncoming wind. If he fell off too far, the boat would heel so hard they would both have to sit on the rail to keep it down. If he could ride through the center of the storm, get past the eye, then maybe he could sail through the other side. They might go in circles, he thought. Please, he prayed, small circles in the middle of the Sound. Not big circles that would take them near the shores.

It was black. Hail was mixed with the rain now; stinging pebbles of ice bruised their skin and skidded into the boat. The wind howled; the shrouds screamed; the waves boomed and crashed. Thunder clapped near and lightning flashed so close they thought they saw it hit the water. This was no nightmare. He would not wake up.

170

"Why didn't you run?" she kept sobbing. And he didn't
—couldn't—answer her. He had made the choice alone.
He had made it instinctively. But if they survived, the
choice would make him free. If they survived, somehow he
would make her understand.

They saw the wave at the same time. It came up broadside from the starboard. It swelled, hovered. The rail
dipped in the hollow before the crest.

Water crashed onto them into the boat, deafening them.
There was a shriek of metal snapping. The boom slammed
onto the deck, and onto Paul's shoulder. Then the sail was
all over them, trapping them in the bottom of the rolling,
heaving boat.

They fought to get free of the clinging wet Dacron
blanket, clawing at it. Finally Paul got an edge and shoved
it onto the seat.

"Are you all right?" He could see her now, hair and eyes
in rivers, frightened but still sitting next to him in the bottom. The boom lay across the rail, and part of the sail
dragged in the chopping seas. He hauled it into the boat,
managed to detach it from the end of the boom and slide it
off. He picked up the broken piece of wire rope, the halyard, that hung uselessly from the corner of the sail.

The prow pitched up and down, swung wildly with every
wave. Paul took the tiller and the jib sheet. That small
triangle of wet white Dacron was all he had to control their
direction now. It would have to do. He had to keep sailing.

He played the sheet, keeping the jib filled but not taut,
just enough to keep moving. He didn't want to take another
wave broadside. Every time a wave passed, the rudder
came out of the water and he couldn't steer. On the jib
alone the boat tended to turn off the wind. Fighting the
tiller with each wave, each gust, took all his strength and all
his mind. There was nothing left in him to think about his
direction or his decision.

171

When he finally found his voice, he said, "I think we just passed the eye. If we can ride it for a little longer, we'll be out of the worst. Do you think you could bail?" The water in the bottom sloshed over their legs.

She found the bucket under the seat and lifted up a section of floorboard. She spilled almost as much back into the boat as she dumped into the thrashing sea, but it helped. She held back her sobs.

"You're still good crew," he said. "It's the captain I'm worried about."

She smiled. "We're alive, aren't we?"

You're taking me home. After everything, you've decided all by yourself to take me home. I'm more frightened about having to lie and pretend again than I was during the storm.

In spite of everything you've told me, I feel safe with you. That's the only thing I'm not confused about. I have to concentrate on that. If I feel safe with you here, then I shouldn't be afraid to go home. But I am.

It took them all afternoon to begin to dry out. His hands shook every time he tried to tie a knot or adjust the rigging. They kept their life jackets on, as much to stay warm as for safety. They did what they did silently.

When the storm finally passed, he discovered from the birdcage off the starboard bow, that they had indeed blown in small circles. They were less than a day's sail from home. He checked the wind and took a not-too-close northwest tack to start him on the way.

They were lucky the halyard, not the mast, had broken. Luck or skill, they'd never know. Judging stress on the sails

172

and lines was, perhaps, instinctive to an experienced sailor. It's always the weakest connection that breaks first. He was glad he'd reefed the main.

Mary Lou was so quiet. He wanted to hold her. He wanted to comfort her, to tell her what he knew. They *could* make their lives what they wanted when they were sure what they wanted. He'd made it home once, he could do it again.

He kept himself busy. He took the main off the boom. He didn't dare climb the mast in mid-Sound with this chop to try to fix the halyard.

He changed back to the genoa jib so they'd have enough sail. It was big and made the boat move, but he had to watch it every second because without the main the boat veered away from the wind, and heeled too far. They'd had enough excitement for one day.

They sat just touching. He felt her tremble.

"We'll be late, you know. But we'll be home before dark. Your parents don't know where you are."

It was not a question.

"No."

"Will Barb keep them from worrying?"

"Yes."

"Good. Then I'll take you home. It'll be all right. You'll see."

"No. You're wrong." Her hair hung in wet clumps. "I don't want to go home. I don't want him to even have a chance to hurt you again. I won't go through that stuff anymore. I've lied before . . ."

That was when he knew what he had to tell her. And as had happened so often in the past two years, he thought wonderingly, it was Amy who showed him the way.

"People make mistakes," he said. "Maybe he made a mistake. Everyone does now and then. Maybe he knows it."

173

She looked at him, startled, opened her mouth and started to say something, then closed it again. She licked her lips and fingered the scrimshaw ring. "What will you . . . will we do if he makes another mistake?"

"He won't. I'm sure he's not stupid enough to make the same mistake twice. Besides, we won't let him. We're not that stupid either."

"What do you mean?"

"I won't walk out on you again. I made a mistake too."

She was quiet awhile. Then softly she said, "Remember I told you how Daddy used to take me walking in the woods? He didn't say much. We'd sit on a log and I'd ask a lot of questions. 'Hush,' he'd say. 'Hush. Just listen and keep your eyes open.' I didn't know what I was watching or listening for, but after a while I'd begin to hear things, a bird fly from its nest, a pine needle drop. Once I saw a huge spider that had a web almost two feet across wash its face. If I pointed or started to say, 'Look!' Daddy would touch my lips to be silent and hold my pointing finger still. Walking home, he'd say, 'You can't hear or see anything if you make noise yourself.' Maybe it's those times that trained me for sitting still in a sailboat. Maybe Daddy got so bad because he misses those woods. He's so rigid about everything, about what he thinks is right or wrong, but forgetting how he used to be, I was seeing him only as wrong. Maybe I made a mistake too."

He tightened the sail but said nothing. He thought it would have been good to walk the woods with her father.

"What will you do?" she asked him finally. "Will you go back to the carwash?"

"I'm not sure. There's a guy I thought I'd talk to about a job. George somebody. I'll think of his last name. He owns a boatyard. I thought—Jojo thought—he might need some help." He paused. "And I thought I'd finish school."

They heard a motor. A Coast Guard launch was coming

174

toward them. When it was close enough, a man on the boat called, "Need any help?"

Paul waved. "No, no thanks. We'll make it back all right."

"Tough storm. Bunch of boats broke moorings, ended up on the rocks. We've been getting calls from all over. Broken masts. One big one—headed for Block Island, I heard—went down. How'd you lose your main?"

"Halyard broke when we took a big wave. We'll make it on the genny."

"Lucky the halyard and not the mast," he said. "You two must be pretty sharp sailors to have weathered that. Good luck!"

"Thanks." Paul waved him on.

They watched the white boat grow small as it headed east. They rocked in its wake.

Mary Lou turned the scrimshaw ring around. Suddenly she grinned at him, a kid on her way to a birthday party. "I just thought of something."

"What?"

"If you go back to school, we'll graduate in the same class."